CHASING JAGUARS

WILD SURVIVAL

CHASING JAGUARS

MELISSA CRISTINA MÁRQUEZ

SCHOLASTIC INC.

Copyright © 2022 by Melissa Cristina Márquez
Interior illustrations copyright © 2022 by Sarah Mensinga

This book is being published simultaneously
in hardcover by Scholastic Press.

All rights reserved. Published by Scholastic Inc., *Publishers since 1920*. SCHOLASTIC and associated logos are trademarks and/or registered trademarks of Scholastic Inc.

The publisher does not have any control over and does not assume any responsibility for author or third-party websites or their content.

No part of this publication may be reproduced, stored in a retrieval system, or transmitted in any form or by any means, electronic, mechanical, photocopying, recording, or otherwise, without written permission of the publisher. For information regarding permission, write to Scholastic Inc., Attention: Permissions Department, 557 Broadway, New York, NY 10012.

This book is a work of fiction. Names, characters, places, and incidents are either the product of the author's imagination or are used fictitiously, and any resemblance to actual persons, living or dead, business establishments, events, or locales is entirely coincidental.

ISBN 978-1-338-63511-9

10 9 8 7 6 5 4 3 2 1   22 23 24 25 26

Printed in the U.S.A. 40

First printing, April 2022

Book design by Yaffa Jaskoll

Para Tata

I wish you were here to see this—
espero que estés orgullosa de mí.
Te quiero.

PROLOGUE

As my arm went into the wet suit to turn it right side out, I was suddenly met with a jolt of instantaneous and extreme pain. *Ouch!*

When I brought my hand back out, I could see it throbbing slightly and turning reddish near the webbing between my thumb and pointer finger. I rubbed the sore spot to see if I could make the pain go away, but it only made me flinch.

"What's the matter, A?" Feye asked, concern flashing across his face.

"Nothing!" I laughed. "I think I must've run into a jellyfish stinger when diving, and it might've gotten stuck to my suit."

"Leave it to you to get stung by a jellyfish and

not even be in the water," he chuckled, rolling his eyes. He reached over to hand me my gloves. "Put these on so you don't get stung again. You've been zapped by their tentacles before; the pain will go away soon enough."

I wasn't sure . . . This pain felt different.

"Something isn't right," I said. I looked down at my tingling hand once more. It was now a bit more swollen and had a single raised dot on it.

"That's . . . not a jellyfish stinger," Feye said. I looked in my wet suit for a loose thorn or something sharp I might have pricked myself with, while Feye looked around our feet.

"A," Feye said, pointing down near our feet. "Look!"

Scurrying away from us was a small scorpion.

CHAPTER ONE

A jolt of airplane turbulence abruptly woke me from a deep sleep. I rubbed my eyes and checked the time. Finally, the longest plane trip ever would soon be over. We had left Sri Lanka and were on our way to Mexico.

Mi país. Our papá was born in Mexico City. I had spent some of my younger years there, too. When Mr. Savage had told us we would be heading back home, our family was ecstatic. It had been years since we had been able to see our *familia* there. He was even letting us fly in a day early to spend some time with them and celebrate *Día de los Muertos*! And I had overheard *Mamá* say we would get to meet up with our old family friends

Tío Esteban and Titi Diana and our "*primo*" Mateo. Mateo wasn't really our cousin, just like Tío Esteban and Tía Diana weren't our real uncle and aunt—we were just super close to them.

Suddenly, Mr. Savage loomed over us in the aisle, not dressed in his usual attire but instead wearing an expensive-looking sweatsuit.

"Good morning . . . afternoon . . . whatever. I know that today is for pleasure, but I wanted to go over again why we are here," he said in a gruff voice.

"A JAGUAR!" an Australian accent said behind us. Our camera and sound crew were behind us. Mark and Alice, in charge of cameras, looked at our sound producer with amusement dancing in their eyes. Connor was the third youngest of the crew (after Feye and me), and he loved big cats just as much as we did—he even had one tattooed on his arm! But he had a lion, not a jaguar like the one we had been called on to help rescue.

"Yes, Connor, a jaguar," Mr. Savage said without any enthusiasm. He was clearly in a mood . . . Maybe he hadn't slept well?

Probably the guilt, I thought, and I quickly looked Mr. Savage over to see if his clothes had the telltale logo that I knew by heart now. When we were in Sri Lanka, I had found sunglasses in Mr. Savage's belongings with a logo that matched the ones that the poachers we'd seen there and in Cuba had been wearing. In Cuba, the poachers had attempted to steal crocodile eggs, and in Sri Lanka, I'd caught them in the act of trying to "fin nap" an extremely rare Pondicherry shark. They were mixed up with Mr. Savage; I just wasn't sure how. Otherwise, it would have been an unbelievable coincidence for them to have shown up at all our shooting locations wearing gear that matched Mr. Savage's. But I couldn't say anything about it until I had more proof.

Mr. Savage cleared his throat and whipped out his tablet to show us footage of a jaguar limping by a camera, with a trap still around one of its back paws. He had received the video from the scientist Daniela Corrales Gutiérrez, who had dedicated her life to studying these big cats. She had reached out to Mr. Savage in the hopes that our family could help find and rehabilitate this animal. She also was hoping that we could help her improve the relationship between conservationists and the locals, who weren't too fond of the predators lurking around their livestock.

"As I mentioned earlier, Ms. Gutiérrez says the locals largely want the animals to be relocated, but some want to kill any jaguars they see in retaliation for their killed livestock." Mr. Savage gestured to the frozen picture of the injured cat on his iPad. "Exhibit A."

He turned off the screen and tucked it under his arm as he produced our trip pamphlets. Each trip we took as part of the *Wild Survival!* crew, we got a small booklet that gave us all the information we needed to know about the country and the animals we would be encountering.

"It's a bit on the light side," my dad laughed, looking at the few pieces of paper stapled together.

Mr. Savage shrugged. "You're from here. What

could you possibly not know?" he said, and then turned to my mom. "I'm sure you know more than what I found on the internet."

Mom laughed at that. She wasn't from Mexico (she had been born in Puerto Rico, like me), but she lived there for a while and knew pretty much just as much as Dad.

"Anyway, read up on the rancheros if you get a chance before you go meet your friends. I won't be able to go with you since I've got a meeting," he said. "But, crew, you are welcome to go if Julio and Evelyn don't mind," Mr. Savage said, nodding toward our parents. They turned around and gave Alice, Connor, and Mark a big thumbs-up. With that, Mr. Savage walked back down the aisle to his own seat.

I looked outside the window. *A meeting that didn't involve Mom and Dad? That wasn't that unusual . . . right?* I wondered if it had anything to do with the poachers . . .

I glanced at the thin pamphlet and opened it

JAGUAR (*PANTHERA ONCA*)

- Third-largest cat species on our planet. It can weigh up to 250 pounds!
- Looks like a leopard but usually smaller and sturdier.
- They face multiple threats in the wild: poaching, habitat loss, and depletion of prey.

up to see a colorful picture of a jaguar staring back at me.

Another jolt of turbulence brought my thoughts to a halt, and I focused once again on the view outside. Although I couldn't see land quite yet, I knew Mexico was below the endless sea of clouds beneath us. There were all different hues of white, ruffling in ripples as if they were a wedding dress painted by an artist's hand. Closer and closer we came to the ground until the plane landed upon the brightly lit tarmac, wheels kissing earth with a small and joyous bounce.

We were here! Home! As soon as the seat belt sign turned off, Feye and I jumped out of our seats, grabbed our bags, and rushed toward the front of the plane to exit. Which was a bad idea since all the adults took forever and we had to wait by the gate for what felt like ages.

"*¡¡Bienvenidos, familia Villalobos!!*" Tío Esteban, Tía Diana, and Mateo screamed as we came through the frosted automatic sliding doors. What a welcome! Mateo came running toward Feye and me, wrapping us up in a huge double hug. I barely recognized him—his black hair was longer and shaggier than the last time I saw him, and his skin seemed to have gotten a healthy dose of sunshine. His brown eyes crinkled when he smiled and kissed me on the cheek. "A, looking *hermosa* as always," he said as he turned to Feye and winked. Alessi, the daughter of one of the zookeepers back at home, was my best friend, and Mateo was Feye's.

"What happened to the hair, *primo*?" Mateo said, running his hand through what was left of it. "I thought it was some neon color."

"*Los padres*," Feye answered with a roll of his eyes and a mock punch to Mateo's arm.

"Ah, say no more, *amigo*," Mateo laughed.

"*Déjame ver a mis hijos*," cried Titi Diana, grabbing our faces with her hands as Tío Esteban went around introducing himself to the rest of the crew.

"That's my cue to leave. See you tomorrow, my stars." Mr. Savage waved to us as he skipped past our family reunion and blended into the sea of people arriving in our wonderful country.

"Come, come, we have much to do to prepare for *Día de los Muertos*!" Titi Diana said as we all were ushered out of the airport and into their giant van.

"This may sound ignorant . . . but what exactly is *Día de los Muertos*, Diana?" Alice asked.

"*Día de los Muertos* honors the dead with festivals and lively celebrations that combine Indigenous Aztec rituals with Catholicism," she explained.

"That latter one you can thank the Spanish conquistadores for," added my dad.

"And the best food!" Mateo and Feye said in unison. We all laughed and fell into our own catch-up conversations.

When I was little, Mom explained to me and Feye that every atom that makes up our glorious planet is a mixture of graveyards and stardust—that all around us we can see the recycling of life.

"And it's up to us to choose how we see life and death—as something macabre or something joyful," Dad had said.

"Does that mean we can't be sad if we lose someone we love?" Feye had asked.

"No, of course you can!" Dad corrected. "Be sad. Feel those feelings of sadness and maybe even anger. But don't forget to feel the good stuff—the joy you felt whenever you saw them, the comfort you found in their hugs . . . those sorts of things."

That's what I thought of as we wandered the graveyard toward our family. Earlier we had helped Diana, Esteban, and Mateo set up their *ofrenda*, exchanging stories about their loved ones. They even surprised us with pictures of our family to put up since we didn't have any with us.

"*Ofrendas* are an essential part of the Day of the Dead celebrations," said Esteban. "They're altars for remembering, typically including marigolds, candles, food, and pictures of dead loved ones."

All around us, families adorned their loved ones'

headstones with bright yellow marigolds and candles, some placing baskets with the favorite foods of those who were now below our feet. I walked closer to Feye. "Isn't it weird that no other animals have graveyards like humans do?"

He looked at me over the basket he was carrying that was filled with delicious food for our very own loved ones. Diana and Esteban had offered to bring us to our grandparents' gravesites to offer them some gifts, as it had been a while since we had been back to properly celebrate this day of remembrance.

"I never thought of it like that," he whispered. I could see his eyes begin to mist up as we let our feet tread lightly over the ground that was supporting new life—grass and little flowers. The shock of life stood out from the dull gray tombstones.

My eyes looked up from the ground as we all stopped, my eyes resting on the names chiseled into the stones.

DORIS MARÍA CRUZ ALVARADO

JOSEPH ROY VILLALOBOS

Dad's parents.

My heart could hear the sound of both their voices, as if they were right there with me. I looked over at Dad, who was now on his knees delicately laying flowers and candles around them. We all did the same, placing the basket of their favorite foods between the two as we lit the candles and exchanged stories about them.

"I think the thing I miss the most about *Tata* is how she always made you feel like you were the most important person in the world. If you were talking to her, she would stop everything to pay attention to just you," Feye said, wiping his eyes with the backs of his hands. It was the first time we had been here since they'd died, and it was . . . a lot. Mom bent over to kiss his cheek.

"That and her cooking. She made the best *arroz y frijoles*," I added, leaning my head on Feye's shoulder. It was just the four of us now. The crew had felt it best for them to go back to the hotel and leave us to this private family moment. I was grateful.

"And Grandfather. I miss having him at the head of our table, talking about anything and everything," Feye said.

I nodded. "I liked when he let me sit on his special comfy chair!" I laughed as Feye scoffed and said he never got that honor.

I looked around at my family and at my grandparents' photos, a smile creeping up even as tears slid down my face. As we continued to reminisce, I couldn't help but notice that through the tears, we were all laughing and smiling. In fact, as I turned to see other families, I also saw joy on their faces as they brought their loved ones back through words.

"While some believe today opens up a bridge between the 'Land of the Dead' and ours, maybe the real bridge is our memories," Dad said.

I squeezed the hands of my family.

Today we would choose joy.

CHAPTER TWO

We left in the early hours of the morning, kissing Tía Diana and Tío Esteban goodbye. I gave Mateo a giant hug under the blanket of stars above us. As our van tires crunched over the gravel road, I waved goodbye and off we went to our next stop: Sonora.

I hadn't been there in years! Sonora, the second-largest state in Mexico by area, offered the best of everything our country was known for. I remembered the stunning palm-fringed beaches, azure seas, and cactus-dotted desert that was bordered by Arizona and New Mexico.

As the sun began to rise and paint the sky multiple shades of pink, orange, and yellow, my stomach grumbled loudly. Lifting up my backpack, I rustled through my stuff to find something to quiet my tummy down. A *concha* and a few *guayabas* sounded like they would hit the spot, and soon I had a mouthful of each in my cheeks.

Spying the bright orange "Mexico" pamphlet that Mr. Savage had given us, I decided to look through more of it. I glanced up to see Mr. Savage in the driver's seat, humming along to some mariachi music that Dad had found on the radio. Mom was in the second row of the van, chatting with Alice about some sort of makeup brand they both loved, while Connor and Mark both slumped against the windows, eyes closed. Feye was next to me in the last row of the van, and he was busy looking out the window and taking selfies for his "legions of fans."

I rolled my eyes and opened the pamphlet, skipping past the basic jaguar information I had seen yesterday and instead looking through the more in-depth information Mr. Savage had included.

Apparently, the northernmost breeding population of jaguars was right where we were going! And

Sonora not only had a Northern Jaguar Reserve, but was also where a lot of "human-wildlife conflict" was happening. Deforestation was leaving many jaguars with no place to call home and diminishing what they could eat. They had no choice but to go near humans and take advantage of the easy food we pretty much left lying around: scraps in landfills, and penned-up cattle. According to these reports, it seemed that the National Commission of Natural Protected Areas even had to relocate a jaguar near the tourist destination of Playa del Carmen because it was so hungry it was hunting dogs there!

I looked over at our sleeping sound producer and remembered his dog, Duke, that I had rescued from the dog pound in Cuba. I couldn't imagine Duke having to fend off a jaguar for his life . . . How scary!

Using satellite collars, scientists like Señora Gutiérrez were tracking where these big cats went. They also attached video cameras along trees in the forest where jaguars were known to live to see if they could capture any live footage of these animals.

It seemed their conservation efforts were working because—

I smacked Feye's arm in shock. "Hey! What was that for?!" he asked, snapping out of the trance he was in thanks to whatever music he was listening to.

"Have you looked over the pamphlet yet?" I asked. He shook his head, and I thrust my brochure toward him. "It says that the jaguar population here has increased almost twenty percent in the last few years! That scientist we are going to meet estimates there are around five thousand individuals now."

Feye rubbed his arm while he looked at the notes. "And you punched me over this . . . why?"

"Because it's exciting and I couldn't help it and I'm sorry," I blurted out. He laughed.

"You Latinas and your extravagant arm motions," he joked, and I stuck out my tongue at him. He pulled out his own pamphlet, and together we went over the notes, letting the hours go by until our surroundings changed. Gone were the cityscapes and suburban houses, replaced with open rolling fields and mountains, nestled in between wild forests. I rolled down my window to get a whiff of the fresh air, listening to birdcalls echo above.

Mr. Savage turned left onto a long dirt driveway. He drove until we finally saw a red wooden house with a big white door and matching white windows. A rooster perched on the black roof. It let out a frightened squawk as the car kicked up brown dust and we slowed to a stop. I could see two kids, a girl and a boy, peering at us through one of the windows. They looked to be around the same age as Feye and me . . . Who were they?

I looked down at my phone and sighed. No bars. My best friend, Alessi, and I had kept missing each other while texting updates about our adventures, hers at the zoo with her mom, us on the road. Pocketing the phone, I opened the door and jumped down. My white sneakers wouldn't stand a chance in this dirt! Adjusting my favorite purple shirt and jean shorts, I walked to meet my family at the front of the van, where I noticed that the girl and boy had come to the door and opened it up, a woman behind them.

"Hi, there! You must be Daniela." Mr. Savage's voice boomed out, causing the rooster to squawk again and practically fall off the roof. It half flew and half flopped onto the ground in an ungraceful heap before shaking itself off and running away behind the house. The kids giggled, looking up to meet my eyes and smile.

"That's me! Daniela Corrales Gutiérrez, it's *un placer* to meet you," the woman said, smiling radiantly. "These are *mis niños*, Mónica and Leo."

"*Hola,*" the kids said in unison. I extended a hand to Mónica first, who took it and pulled me in for a kiss on each cheek. Of course, silly me! We were home! Here, we kissed cheeks to say hello and goodbye. I always felt awkward meeting new people because I was so used to kissing their cheeks as a greeting, but many people where we now lived preferred a handshake instead. I looked down at our hands, still holding on to each other, and noticed that her caramel skin tone matched mine. In fact, our hair was almost the same color, except hers was a bit darker and straighter. I looked to her brother, who was giving Feye a fist bump, and to their mom. They were all definitely related—they looked like carbon copies of one another!

"If you're thinking, *Gee, they look alike*, it's because we're twins," Leo said, watching me as my eyes looked from one to the other. "I'm the oldest, though—by three minutes!"

"We're both fourteen, Leo. Get off your high horse," Mónica laughed, jabbing her finger into her brother's ribs. I knew that move—I had done it to Feye (and been on the receiving end) multiple times!

Leo came forward and gave me a kiss on the cheek. "Welcome. Have you been to Sonora before?"

We nodded.

"Come inside, you must be hungry. We have some breakfast cooking and we can talk about what is going on here over some good food," Daniela said, ushering us up the porch steps and into her home.

We were all instantly hit with amazing scents—a combination of savory and earthy notes mixed with fresh herbs, vegetables, and generous amounts of citrus. As we made our way to the kitchen, we were stopped in our tracks by the beautiful presentation before us. This was why Mexican food was one of my favorite cuisines. The blend of different cultures, the spices and seasonings used, the vibrant colors that invited you to take multiple helpings . . . it was all just part of what made this food so irresistible.

"Grab a plate and help yourself! *Buen provecho.*" Daniela smiled, grabbing herself a plate and piling on some freshly made corn tortillas. Tortillas are the building blocks of Mexican food, eaten at practically every meal and made into several staples: taquitos, tostadas, quesadillas, enchiladas, flautas, and more. And I spied a few of those in this spread! Feye pushed me aside to quickly get to the huevos rancheros, one of our favorite meals, and I could see Mom happily helping herself to a large portion of chilaquiles.

Once at the table, my stomach growled at the different smells: garlic, onions, cilantro, oregano, cumin, and chilies. We were all quiet for a few minutes, happily eating. It wasn't until after we all got another helping of food (or third helping, if you were Connor) that Alice suggested we talk about what was going on in the town so she and Mark could start filming segments for the show.

"As you may know, I'm a wildlife biologist who works within the Northern Jaguar Reserve here to protect its dwindling jaguar population. These powerful cats used to roam Latin American jungles, but they have been hunted for sport, their gorgeous pelts, and the threat they pose to cattle," Daniela explained, pausing to take a sip of water.

"They used to be trapped and poisoned by hunters who were paid by the federal government," Leo elaborated, now done with his plate of food and going around to collect the other empty ones.

"Exactly right, Leo." Daniela smiled. "This town is full of rancheros whose livelihoods depend on their cattle. Unfortunately, they are right at the edge of the reserve, and the jaguars have killed a few of their animals because they are hungry. While most rancheros want them to be relocated to a different part of the reserve, someone has taken it upon themself to set up some nasty traps."

"Like the one in the video and pictures you sent us?" my dad asked, looking to Mr. Savage to give him the tablet with the evidence. Dad pulled the video up and showed us the injured jaguar again.

"*Pobrecito*," cried Mónica.

"It looks like someone may want to kill any jaguars they see in retaliation for their dead livestock, but obviously that is a big assumption to make. I don't have enough evidence to point any fingers. I wouldn't dare accuse anyone of this," Daniela said, her eyes glued to the picture of the sad-looking predator. "I'm hoping that your family can find this animal, rehabilitate it, and help us reach out to the community about this sensitive topic."

"Us?" Mark asked, putting down his cup of

steaming hot *café*. Hot tendrils curled up from the porcelain mug. Even though I didn't drink coffee, I had to admit it looked yummy!

"A team of fellow conservationists and I live here to not only study and protect the jaguars, but to improve relationships between these predators and the people who call this area home. We're scientists . . . you're superb science communicators . . . We thought it would be a good collaboration. Plus, the television show will allow others around the world to admire Latin America's jaguars!"

Mr. Savage bounced up from his chair. "I can see it now," he exclaimed, hands out in front of him as if he were filming right that second. "The episode will be called 'Chasing Jaguars.' We can set up camera traps around the forest for constant surveillance to find these fearsome predators. We need to locate this injured one and save its life! The Villalobos family, heroes once again. And we can tranquilize one, get up close and personal with it, do some science . . . stuff . . . and then we'll see where it goes."

His head whipped over to Alice. "Are you taking notes? We need killer shots of it getting gruesome with some cattle or something else in the forest. We need bait. Can we get bait here? Oh, and we need . . . Come on, you lot, let's walk and talk." Mr. Savage motioned for the camera crew to get up and join him as he continued to ramble on about the shots he needed for the show.

Daniela looked after them and then turned back to us. "Is he always this . . ."

"Enthusiastic? Yes, *amiga*." My mom laughed.

"Well, I can help with the 'science stuff,' since we just got a shipment of thirty new camera traps to set up around the area." Daniela pointed to a box in the next room over that said FRAGILE: CAMERAS in bright red lettering.

"If he wants to track one, we'll need some collars," Mom said.

"Hopefully not an ugly pet collar," Feye joked.

"No, it's a special collar that allows scientists to better monitor and understand jaguar behavior by using satellite technology," Mónica corrected. She grabbed something off the nearby shelf and showed it to our family. It looked like a dog collar you could find at the local pet store, but with an antenna coming out of it on one side and a plastic-looking box on the other side. "These give hourly updates on their movements for up to eight months. *Mami* and her team get a whole heap of data back to show how they use the forest to live."

Feye visibly blushed. It wasn't often a girl showed him up when it came to animal knowledge. "Cool," he said, and looked away from Mónica's brown-eyed gaze.

Yeah . . . he liked her.

Just then Mr. Savage came rushing back in, his pale face flushed pink. "I don't want us to track down just any jaguar, Evelyn. I want the one they call El Jefe!"

"Good luck!" Leo laughed, his hand quickly covering his mouth in the realization that we'd all heard him. Mr. Savage gave him a glare.

Daniela was also giving him the universal "mom look," which meant he would be getting a stern talking-to later. After a few tense seconds, she turned back toward us.

"Who . . . or what . . . is El Jefe, Rick?" my dad asked, a little exasperated. Was this another one of Mr. Savage's ploys to get a "monster animal" on the show?

"A famous male jaguar who crossed from Mexico into the United States. He has a craft beer named after him—he has murals! People love him!" Mr. Savage said.

"They also demonize him as a 'Mexican intruder,'" Daniela interrupted, her eyes narrowed. "I won't be a part of something that wants to paint him, or any other jaguar, in a bad light."

Mr. Savage was quiet for a second. "Fine," he said at last. "But collaring a rare black jaguar would suffice, then."

He went back out into the other room with the crew, and Daniela gave us a wink. "Now I agree with him . . ."

We laughed, breaking the friction in the room. I hadn't really seen anyone stand up to Mr. Savage like that! Sure, my parents had, but most people kind of let him do what he wanted if it meant being on television.

"You said not all rancheros were on board with relocating the jaguars. Can I ask who isn't keen?" my mom said. Daniela nodded and motioned for us to follow her. Out the front door we went, and she pointed to a house far in the distance on her right.

"The majority of ranchers and the community want to coexist with these jaguars. But one ranchero, who is like the town figurehead, is someone I have not been able to persuade just yet," Daniela said. "His name is Señor José Ramón Velásquez. He was one of the hunters paid off by the government all those years ago, actually. Not to mention his cattle are the ones getting eaten because he lives just on the outskirts here."

"He sets out traps and shoots into the forest at night whenever he thinks he hears a jaguar come near his cattle," Leo explained. I nodded and squinted, barely making out the small blue house. I could easily see the animals, though.

"I say we go pay him a visit, then," Mr. Savage said from behind us, startling us all at his sudden appearance.

He brushed past us and started marching down the very long driveway. We all looked at one another, shrugged, and followed.

CHAPTER THREE

*B*ANG! BANG! BANG!

"Knock, knock! Is anyone in *la casa*?" Mr. Savage said. He was slightly panting from the long walk in the hot morning sun. We all were—I could feel my shirt sticking to my back, and Feye was smelling a *little* stinky. I saw him give himself a quick whiff and stand a bit farther apart from Mónica.

First the blush and now being self-conscious? Feye definitely had a crush.

"Maybe he went out with his family for breakfast, Rick," Dad said.

"On a Tuesday?" Mr. Savage huffed. He raised his hand to knock on the aged wooden door again when it flew open. There in front of us stood a man not much taller than Mr. Savage. The hair under his cowboy hat was snow white, a stark contrast to his coffee-colored skin and piercing blue eyes. Even his bushy white mustache didn't hide the thin line his lips were creating.

"He doesn't seem too happy to see us," Feye whispered to me.

"Yeah, you think?" I whispered back.

"Ah! *Buenos días, señor.* How are—" Mr. Savage started, but the old man looked past him and at Ms. Daniela instead.

"*¿Daniela, qué es esto?* You are now ambushing me in the morning to talk about your stupid cats?" he said in a deep, gruff voice. It seemed as weathered as his skin.

"*Perdón*, Señor José, but this man wanted to discuss the jaguars with you. He is a television producer for the *familia* Villalobos here." Ms. Daniela motioned to us and we all awkwardly waved.

He hesitated, then nodded at us. "*Hola. Mucho gusto.* The kids, Leo and Mónica, have seen your videos on the computer and told me you were coming." We turned around to look at the twins, who shrugged.

"We help Señor José around the ranch while his family is away," Leo explained.

"I'm really good at rounding up the cattle!" Mónica said proudly.

Señor José looked at me. "I heard you got bitten by some big lizard."

I pointed to my leg, where the scars were. "Yeah, a crocodile."

He moved a little closer to look, nodded, then straightened himself up to look at Leo and Mónica. "You promised to help today. Are you here to do that or talk about this cat?"

"We can do both," Mónica suggested. Señor José made a noise that sounded like *pfft*.

"I don't want to talk about the cat with this man. I have too much work to finish today," Señor José muttered.

"We can help!" I volunteered.

"We can?" Feye asked. I nodded. "We know how to ride horses. We don't know anything about rounding up cattle, but we're quick learners. Right, *hermano*?"

Feye looked at Mónica, who was giving us an enthusiastic thumbs-up. He quickly nodded. "Yup, sure can learn! Real quick!"

Señor José seemed to ponder this for a second. "*Bueno*. If all the work gets done, I am happy to talk about the big kitty . . . tomorrow."

"And would you be willing to have the conversation on camera?" Mr. Savage asked, a big smile plastered on his face.

Señor José did a double take.

"It would be perfect for this 'Chasing Jaguars' episode. We could have the local ranchers come together and talk about what you all can do about the jaguar *problema* you seem to find yourself in," Mr. Savage explained.

Señor José eyed Mr. Savage up and down, then looked at Daniela, who was looking at him expectantly.

He gave a curt nod and opened the door to his home, giving a *"Siéntense"* command to three cattle dogs, who immediately sat.

While Señor José gave tasks to the adults to help with, Mónica and Leo took us outside to where a barrel with horns stood. Mónica handed Feye a coiled rope, keeping one for herself. "Before you round up cattle, you need to learn how to catch one," she said.

"So what *mi hermana* has is rope that has been tied on one end like a circle. That's called the lasso and that's what we use to catch runaway cattle," Leo explained.

"Oh! We use something similar for the big animals at our zoo," I said, looking at the rope.

"Now, don't hold your wrist stiffly. Let it move easily around as you swing the lasso over your head," Señor José said from behind us. We all turned around to watch him demonstrate how to perfectly cast the lasso onto the barrel. "Swing it above your head three times, then throw it. Point your finger right where you want the rope to go."

Feye gave it a try. The rope sailed toward the barrel, but it didn't wrap around like Señor José's did. He motioned for me to try next and I had the same result.

"Practice makes perfect. You two keep it up. Mónica and Leo, *¿están conmigo?*" Señor José instructed. We ran back and forth to collect our crumpled-up ropes until Feye cried out, "*¡Lo hice!* I did it, look!" as his rope easily made its way around the barrel.

We hollered and cheered, high-fiving one another. When Mónica congratulated him, he smiled shyly and I stuck my tongue out at him.

I couldn't get the perfect lasso, no matter how long and hard I tried. By the afternoon, my arms were tired. I wondered if the next cast would be my lucky one when Ms. Daniela whistled and told everyone we were done and heading home. Señor José shook her hand and told us all *gracias*.

"See you all tomorrow for the community meeting."

A weak cheer passed through the camera crew. Mr. Savage looked positively exhausted, even though I only saw him lugging around one hay bale the entire time we were there.

"Being a ranchero is hard work!" Mark sighed, clapping his hands together to shake the dust off. I tidied up the ropes and handed them back to Señor José, who clasped a sturdy hand on my shoulder. "Cheer up. You'll get it soon enough."

Once we were back at Daniela's home, Mr. Savage and the camera crew headed outside to the backyard to go over the game plan for tomorrow.

In the guest bedroom that I shared with Feye, I opened my suitcase and took out the camera my *tata* had given me as a gift recently. If I could remember to keep the lens cap off, I was hoping to get a picture of a jaguar! I placed it near my pillow . . . just in case. It couldn't hurt to be prepared.

CHAPTER FOUR

Loud barking startled me awake. My eyes tried to focus in the darkness as I realized it wasn't even daylight yet. My fingers splayed out, looking for my phone to use as a flashlight. The numbers "02:35" greeted me, as did the background picture of Alessi and me with a baby penguin from the zoo.

More barking. *What was going on out there?* Still in my pajamas, I slipped on my sneakers and made my way to the living room, where everyone stood, also in their pajamas.

"What's happening?" I asked, rubbing the sleep from my eyes as adrenaline coursed through my body. I was alert, even though my brain really wanted me to go back to sleep.

"The guard dogs at Señor José's ranch are barking at something. I'm going to check it out," Daniela said as she grabbed her car keys and made her way out the front door.

"It might be some jaguar action! Follow her! Mark, you have your camera?" Mr. Savage commanded as he practically pushed us out the door.

Mark smirked, eyeing the camera by his side. *Of course* he had his camera.

The drive over was quick since Mr. Savage didn't seem to think speed limits existed in the middle of the night in this otherwise-sleepy town. Others had also heard the racket, and cars littered Señor José's driveway. Our headlights illuminated his expansive yard. We could see him unleashing his dogs, their paws tearing at the soft dirt as they chased an unknown threat.

"Señor José, what is happening? *¿Qué sucedió?*" Daniela cried out. She turned around and walked toward us, her eyes watching the dogs disappear into the darkness. I looked up from the forest to see a dazzling array of stars watching from above, cushioned like sparkling diamonds in the velvet night.

He opened his mouth to answer but a loud noise got all our attention. A deafening roar, followed by barks, came from the direction the dogs had gone.

"Jaguar. Spooked some of my calves and a few jumped the fence. *Ayúdame*," Señor José said as he loaded his gun. "Do any of you city folks know how to use a gun?"

Mr. Savage immediately stepped up. "I do." Señor José passed him a rifle and some ammo.

"You can't shoot it!" my mom said, wrapping herself up in her arms to brace against the cold. I shivered, but not because of the cold—because I hated thinking about an animal getting hurt when we were here to protect it. Dad brought my mom close and pressed a kiss onto her forehead.

"We have to do something," he replied before motioning to a growing group of people. All of them had red-light torches on their heads so they could see their surroundings without spooking anything around them. Mark and his camera followed, the red light blinking to let us know that whatever was about to happen would be recorded for the whole world to possibly see.

"*Niños*, stay here," my parents and Daniela all said at the same time, leaving me, Feye, Mónica, and Leo by the car. I could hear them trying to plead with the rancheros to shoot up in the air to scare the jaguar away instead of hurting it. Another roar came from the forest, this time farther away.

And then . . . quiet. Even the crickets, which had been chirping softly in the background, had gone mute. It was as if the whole area were holding its breath to see what would happen next.

A cold wind rustled the leaves around us, and Mónica huddled up closer to Feye, who hesitated before putting an arm around her. I crossed my arms in front of me, rubbing them to keep myself warm. What was taking them so long?

"Do . . . do you think they're in trouble?" Leo

whispered, as if afraid to speak any louder and break the tension around us. Or maybe he was just tired.

"I think they're okay. There are a lot of them," Feye replied.

Worry was etched on all our faces, both for our families and for the jaguar.

A *BANG!* tore through the quiet, causing us all to flinch. One more followed, and then the silence wrapped around us once again. I couldn't help but be transported back to the last time I had heard a gunshot, when Mr. Savage had killed the crocodile that had bitten me. I shuddered. Were we about to witness another animal death?

The minutes felt like hours, but eventually the search party returned, their eyes filled with disappointment and ... something else I couldn't quite put a finger on.

When I spotted my parents, I tore away from the group to give them a hug. They bent down and wrapped me up between them, and that's when I noticed my mother's face was damp with tears.

"What happened?" I asked. "Did they kill the jaguar?" My heart felt like it was breaking.

She shook her head. "No, *mi vida*. But it got one of the calves and Señor José had to put it down."

As if on cue, Señor José and Mr. Savage emerged from the forest carrying something between them I couldn't quite see. Dad picked me up effortlessly from *Mami*'s embrace, my arms wrapping around his sweaty neck as he brought me over near Feye. "Stay here. You don't need to see this," he said. From beyond his shoulder I could see them lay down the calf in the illuminated backyard.

"Get in the car, everyone. We'll be going home soon," Daniela said, opening the door to her car for us, which was parked in front of the van we had taken to get here. Leo sat up front, while Mónica, Feye, and I sat in the back. She closed the door and went back to my parents, Mr. Savage, and Señor José, who were all talking about something as Mark filmed them from a distance.

My eyes wandered back to the calf, lying on its

side in the middle of the yard. The other cattle had begun to moo, almost as if in mourning. We sat there listening before Feye cleared his throat and spoke, looking directly at me.

"I love big cats, you know I do . . ." he started. "And I want to see them properly protected and living wild and free, like they used to. But I can definitely understand why these rancheros want to protect their livelihood."

As the cars began to peel away from the driveway, leaving the scene of the crime one by one, I couldn't help but notice that each of the passengers was frowning and looking frustrated at another death caused by the jaguars. Truth was . . . I agreed with Feye. And it was that thought that haunted me as I made my way back to my bed and closed my eyes, the jaguar roar and sad cow moos still ringing in my ears.

CHAPTER FIVE

Dad, Feye, and Leo were setting up tables and chairs for the community meeting while *Mamá*, Mónica, Daniela, and I were inside making tamales. We filled corn husks with meats, beans, and even cheese. I snuck a few bites of cheese without anyone noticing.

I remembered first learning how to make home-made tamales with our nanny, Señora Inés, when our parents had to leave us at home to go on big trips. She was a sweet, elderly woman who had the most gorgeous singing voice and loved us as if we were her own. Señora Inés made incredible tamales, and she taught us how to make her masa completely from scratch using dried white corn kernels.

My attention turned back to this latest batch of dough beneath my fingers, ready to be spread on the presoaked corn husk, filled with delicious red chili pork and broth, and then cooked.

"Adrianna, *mi tesoro*, you must go faster than one tamale every ten minutes if we are going to make enough for everyone to eat!" *Mamá* joked, her hip pushing against mine to bring me back to reality.

"*Sí, Mami.* I know, sorry," I said, folding one long side of the husk over the filling, then the other, and then tying the tamales. The water on the stove was already boiling, ready to add the tamales, but first Daniela had to fish out the coin that was placed at the bottom. When the coin started tapping the pot, that was when you knew the water was ready.

With a satisfying little plop, I added my tamales to the pot of water that already had some standing up, thanks to Mónica's quick hands. *Música* drifted in and out of the kitchen from an old radio. The sound of a mariachi band had us all humming along while the guys chatted about chair placements.

"Julio! We're almost done here if you want to start your salad," my mom called out from the open kitchen window. I could see Connor had joined them outside since Mark, Alice, and Mr. Savage were in the forest with Señor José to film where they had found the calf.

"Coming, dear! Hey, Adrianna," Dad said, clasping a hand on my arm. "You like to cook. Let me show you your dad's secret recipe."

Dad instantly took up a good third of the bench space to make his famous jicama salad with mango, cilantro, lime, black beans, and rice. He talked me through each step and why the flavors worked together so well.

A knock on the front door alerted us to the guests beginning to arrive. The men each wore a sombrero bearing their farm's name, as if it was a planned way of identifying one another. Some rancheros had brought their whole families, while others just came with their spouse or alone. As people trickled in, we kids were tasked with bringing food out to the lunch table.

"Alright, *buen provecho* to everyone. Dig in!" Daniela said as she brought out the last of the hot tamales and placed them in the center of the long table. Dishes and cutlery clattered as people piled their plates high with the delicious food, their voices murmuring thanks to one another for passing a dish their way or expressing appreciation to us for cooking it all.

Once everyone was seated and had enjoyed at least a little of their food, Daniela opened up the table for discussion about the "jaguar situation," as she called it. Unsurprisingly, Señor José was the first to stand up.

"I understand that it is tough for the *gatos* since they have less habitat, but what about us? We, too, are struggling to survive in these remote, mountainous deserts of Sonora!" he said, looking around for other rancheros to back him up.

I looked around at the different faces to see some of them nodding solemnly and one younger couple shaking their heads. "May we?" the man asked Daniela, who nodded. Señor José shot them a glare as he sat down.

"Does Señor José not like them?" I leaned over to ask Leo, who sat on my left. He shook his head and whispered, "Not at all. That's Mr. Jorge Ballesteros and his wife, Mrs. Dora—they're kind of new."

I looked at the couple who now stood up. The woman's heart-shaped face was framed with long black hair that cascaded down her back in soft curls. Mr. Jorge's hand rested on her back, his olive skin in contrast to her pale complexion. His shaggy black hair bobbed up and down as he nodded to whatever his wife was saying, brown eyes that matched hers fully focused on her lips as she spoke.

"The jaguars were here first—they're struggling to survive against decades of hunting," she said, capping off the end of her passionate speech. I couldn't help but nod along with her.

"You can't tell me this isn't my home! My family has been here for generations!" Señor José spat back, his hands hitting the table so hard that even our plates and cups down at the end of the table shook.

"And we can respect that, José, but they've been here for even longer," Mr. Jorge said. "Look, attacking livestock is a natural behavior for these carnivores—just how seeking to protect your livestock is similarly a natural reaction."

"Well, I'm glad we agree on that," Señor José said, crossing his arms.

Mrs. Dora ignored him, going on to say how the traditional attitudes that rancheros held toward the jaguars had been changing, morphing instead into newfound pride and respect for the animals.

"Well, I'm not respecting them!" Señor José interrupted. "They are robbing me of money. One of my cattle is their breakfast but it is part of my family's livelihood." Many of the ranchers murmured in agreement.

Daniela stood up to speak. "Look, as a professional in big-cat conservation, I understand that point of view, and that is why we are here having this conversation. I want to work together with everyone to show that ranching and jaguars can coexist here."

"And how do you plan on doing that?" Señor José asked warily.

"By basically tucking your cattle in at night, for starters," Daniela said. I looked again toward Leo to see if he understood what his mom was saying. Surely, she wasn't talking about giving each cow a bed and blanket and telling them good-night stories . . . right?

"Not literally," Leo clarified. "She means rounding them up during the afternoon and having them penned up in a night corral. Some of the ranchers here already do that, and they also have some tame water buffalo in their group since they're territorial and will help deter jaguars."

"By making sure the fences are fixed, corralling the young, pregnant, and sick cows, and keeping

WATER BUFFALO

- Water buffalo can be domestic or wild. Very few wild water buffalo remain, but there are multiple breeds of domestic water buffalo in the world.
- Domestic water buffalo are especially well adapted for tilling rice fields.
- There are over 130 million water buffalo spread across the world.

your animals in those enclosures, it will substantially reduce the jaguar predation rates," Daniela continued. "Meaning your cows are safe, you save money in the long run, and the jaguars don't face any retaliation."

It sounded easy enough. But like all conservation issues, this problem involved humans, and that made things a little trickier. I had learned my lesson in Sri Lanka. Even though the solution seemed easy, I had to consider the real people who lived nearby. I knew that one person's opinion could derail all the hard work put into a solution.

I looked up at Daniela with admiration; as a wildlife scientist and conservationist, she not only had to be a good communicator but also a really good listener. I was still working on the second part. My mom and dad had found their calling and audience in front of the camera. Feye had social media. I was figuring it out, but I knew one thing: I wanted to be just like Daniela someday.

Daniela started to talk about the importance of

the camera traps and satellite tags she and her team were wanting to put on the local jaguars. I turned to face Señor José. While he was no longer glaring at the Ballesteros family, he still didn't look entirely pleased or persuaded by what Daniela was saying.

"Let's implement this technology and these strategies for a little while to see if they are effective against jaguars," Daniela pleaded. "Could you at least promise me, Señor José, you won't just blindly shoot the next one you see?"

The table was quiet as all eyes turned to the old man, who now leaned forward in his seat as he mulled over her request.

"I can promise I will try, and that's all," he finally said. "Let's see what science can do to help us."

CHAPTER SIX

The sun felt warm on my face as we arrived in the luscious green forest with the whole crew the next morning. Daniela, Leo, and Mónica were already there with Mr. Savage setting up the props we would be using for today's segment. I was going to learn how to capture jaguars and tag them! Fortunately, no glue was involved with this tagging process . . . When we were on location in Cuba, I had accidently glued Feye's hand to a live crocodile!

"First, let's talk about what camera trapping is," Daniela said into the camera. "It's a survey tool that scientists use to learn more about the life history of animals."

"Great, Daniela," Mr. Savage said. "But we have

plenty of you in the show. How about giving one of your kiddos some of the limelight?" He looked at Leo and said, "How would you like to be a star, kid?"

Leo looked at his mom, who nodded. "You know this equipment, too, sweetie."

He grabbed one of the camera trap setups from the nearby table and brought it over to use as a prop.

"Look at this—he's a natural!" Mr. Savage crooned. "Now pretend you're explaining it to Feye and Adrianna. Mark, get close to this. Alice, get a wider shot."

Leo waited for his cue from Mr. Savage to start talking. "This is a remotely activated camera equipped with a trigger. It's left in the field to capture images of animals when researchers aren't around," Leo said, smiling at me as the cameras kept rolling. "These use infrared sensors." Mark's camera zoomed in as Leo's fingers went over the different parts.

"Hey, Mónica, do you wanna be a star, too?" Mr. Savage asked over his shoulder, his voice carrying to where she stood by Connor and his overhead microphone. She shook her head, clearly not a fan of being in front of the camera.

"Suit yourself. Leo, continue." Mr. Savage shrugged.

"But camera traps aren't the only technology we use," Leo said, and looked to his mom, who smiled at him.

"That's right, Leo! We also use satellite tags. These tags allow scientists like myself to study the individual behavior of jaguars and determine the exact routes they take," Daniela explained. "That way we know what parts of a specific region are really being used by local populations and highlight them as areas to be protected."

"Adrianna knows all about satellite tags," Feye said in a dramatic tone.

I elbowed him. "*Hermano*, I promise not to glue you to a jaguar," I said as the crew chuckled.

Mr. Savage shook his head and pointed at Daniela to continue.

"Camera traps and satellite tags help researchers monitor threatened species populations as a whole," Daniela said. "We are so happy to announce that thanks to the network that sponsors *Wild Survival!*, we have been able to buy twenty satellite tags that will allow us to gather crucial jaguar population data here." She ended by holding up one of the tags in her hand.

"So how do we get one of these tags on such an elusive animal?" Dad asked, Alice's camera panning over to him.

"Leo and I are going to show you how we lure, trap, and tag the jaguars here!" Daniela smiled.

Leo ran offscreen to grab a camera trap. "Mounting these on trees is easy—just make sure to point the camera down to the ground so you don't miss anything!" he said, jogging back toward us.

"The next stage is to catch several jaguars and fit them out with transmitters. This will enable us to track the wandering of individuals," Daniela said. "But before a tracking collar can be placed on a jaguar, it has to be caught. Thanks to the cameras, we will know the areas where the chances of catching one are best."

"Paths and dirt roads crisscross this forest, and jaguars use them as an easy way to move from one point to another," Leo explained, motioning down to our feet, where the ground was flatter than that beside us. "Mom and her team block other paths out with branches so the jaguar has to step in a certain area . . . where the snare is!"

He ran offscreen again, this time bringing back with him a dead chicken and a snare. After living at a zoo, bait like this no longer threw me off. It wasn't exactly pleasant, but it was part of the job. Feye and I had a lot in common with the twins, and it was nice to be around kids our age who understood our weird reality. "Sometimes we have bait to lure the jaguar to a certain spot," Leo said.

"Right, Leo! And we have a spring-loaded platform that is triggered when a jaguar steps on it, allowing for this flexible loop to then tighten around one of their legs. That keeps it in place until I, or other researchers, can arrive," said Daniela.

"But how long does it stay there?" I asked, wondering if the poor jaguars would be stuck for hours. "How do you know if the snare has something?"

"The snare is linked to a radio transmitter, so we are alerted when an animal has been trapped," Daniela responded.

"But is it always a jaguar in the snare?" Mom asked, looking at the snare that Daniela was now passing around. I knew she knew the answer to the question, but that's why she was so good at this. She knew it was something the audience was probably wondering.

"Not always." Daniela shook her head. "Sometimes we get other animals snared in the trap. Even if it's not a jaguar, we still have to tranquilize it with a dart before we can free it."

"What does this tranquilizer dart look like?"

Feye asked. This time, it was Daniela who retrieved the tool. The camera followed her as she showed off the bright orange dart.

"So, if it is a jaguar in the trap, you shoot the jaguar with this tranquilizer dart," Dad said. "And then what?"

"We wait until it's safe for us to examine it, and then half the team works on getting the transmitting collar on and making sure it works, while the other part of the team examines the sedated jaguar," Daniela explained, holding up a piece of equipment that kind of looked like an air conditioner remote. "For example, this is a device that measures its pulse and its blood oxygen levels."

"How?" Feye asked, walking over to look at the device.

"See this blue cord and clip?" Daniela asked, and Feye nodded. "We put this clip on its tongue to measure that!"

"Whoa!" I said, running over to look at the fancy piece of equipment. It looked like Daniela was about to say something, but suddenly an abrasive sound stopped the words right on her tongue.

"Cut! Perfect," Mr. Savage bellowed. A tree rustled overhead as birds fled from his loud voice. "Here's the game plan: I want the scientists to come with the camera crew and see if we can tag a jaguar."

"What about the kids?" Mom asked, motioning toward us.

"They can go ahead and find some of the camera traps and switch the cameras out since the batteries don't last that long," Mr. Savage said, waving us to go off in a general direction. "Leo, kid, you have a map to where the cameras that need switching are, right?"

Leo nodded.

"There ya go!" Mr. Savage said, smiling at my mom. "Everyone is kept busy."

"But it's a family show, Rick," Dad insisted. "If we tag the jaguar, it should be together."

"And I'm telling you this is what I want them to do 'cause . . ." Mr. Savage paused, as if he was looking for what was probably an excuse to not have us poking around. "Adrianna doesn't exactly have a good track record with tagging," he said in a hushed voice.

My cheeks burned red, partly with embarrassment but also because I was upset. I tried to interject, but Mr. Savage continued.

"Oi, Alice! Give them the smaller cameras to capture stuff while they're out," Mr. Savage instructed, waving toward the van to get the "Villalobos Vision" cameras he had been giving Feye and me whenever we went on solo adventures.

With a roll of her eyes toward his gruff voice, Alice did what she was told and tinkered around with both cameras to make sure they worked properly before handing them over.

"You guys know what you're doing." Alice winked as she gave one to Feye and one to me. We winked back as she headed over to her camera and picked it up over her strong shoulders.

"See? Everyone will be on camera!" Mr. Savage

said to Dad. He herded our parents, Daniela, and the rest of the camera crew toward the forest, impatiently snapping his fingers for Alice to hurry up.

"Capture us something good, kids!" Mr. Savage said as he and the adults disappeared into the woods.

CHAPTER SEVEN

The first three camera traps were easy to switch out. There was no evidence of jaguars having been near them recently, and I was anxious we wouldn't have anything exciting to capture on our Villalobos Vision cameras.

At the start of our walk, I had managed to get a quick video of some military macaws, but the footage was shaky, and I knew it wouldn't be usable.

"Don't worry, *amigos*," Mónica said, probably because of my worried face. "This next camera is one we usually get a lot of activity on!"

"Really?" I asked her.

"I've got a good feeling about it," she said, giving me a small smile.

MILITARY MACAW

- This colorful bird gets its name from the way its feather pattern resembles a military parade uniform.
- The military macaw is native to forest regions in Mexico and South America.
- Their life span is 50 to 60 years long, and they live in large flocks.

"You and your feelings, *hermana*," Leo said, looking back at us from in front of the group. "You can't go by gut feelings! You got to go with proof."

"What kind of proof, Leo?" his twin replied with a sly smile on her face.

"Well, tracks, for one," he replied, and then said "Aha!" when he spotted the last camera mounted up on a thick tree's trunk. He ran ahead to grab it, Feye filming the whole thing on the Villalobos Vision camera so that we would at least have some sort of action for the show.

"Jaguar tracks, just to be clear?" Mónica asked, the smile still on her face. I looked at her and she winked at me, a twinkle in her eyes. *What was she up to?*

"Yeah, of course. Chicken tracks won't tell us a jaguar is nearby, Sis," Leo scoffed.

"Mmm . . . hmm . . . hey, Leo?" Mónica said. "Look down."

Leo was standing next to a singular, humongous paw print embedded in the soft earth. It was almost as big as his shoe—no ordinary house cat did that!

His head snapped up to look at us as his mouth fell open. "Oh my gosh!"

"I always trust my gut feelings." Mónica smiled.

"Yeah, yeah," Leo said, putting his hand next to the paw print to get an idea of how big the jaguar was.

"Look!" Feye said, pointing to more of them going in a direction ahead of us. "They seem fresh, so it must mean a jaguar is nearby!"

I squealed with excitement. *Was I about to see a jaguar in the wild?!*

"How do you know they're fresh?" I asked.

Feye bent down to the closest paw print next to him and pointed around the edges of it. "One of the best ways to figure out if a track is fresh or not is to look for clearly defined edges. Wind and rain can wash them away, and they'll fade the more time passes. These are super defined . . . meaning they have to be fresh."

Leo was no longer paying attention and charged ahead, urging us to follow him and the tracks. "It must be nearby! Let's go find a big kitty!"

Feye and I looked at each other and shrugged. We fell into step behind Leo as he made up a story of what he thought this particular jaguar was doing here. The minutes dragged on as we followed each huge paw print, yet we found no other trace of the animal that had left it behind.

"And the tracks just stop here." Leo sighed, pointing to the last tracks that ended at the base of an old tree. "Well, that was a waste of time!"

"What did you expect to find, Leo, a jaguar eating a feral pig on the ground?" Feye teased.

"Actually, yes," Leo replied.

"You guys . . . look up!" Mónica gasped, pointing up the trunk of the tree we now stood under. It took a moment for my eyes to adjust to the contrasting sunshine and treetop shade, but there, in all its glory, was a resting jaguar.

"Whoa!" Feye breathed, and instantly his phone was in his hands, snapping pictures and trying to capture the immense cat. Its eyes were closed. I was surprised by how well the gorgeous leopard-like rosettes had initially camouflaged the jaguar. Speechless, I took my own phone out and snapped a picture of it draped across the tree branch. After the third one, an alert said that my battery was low, but I clicked ignore and kept taking photos.

"It kind of looks like that El Jefe jaguar Mr. Savage was talking about earlier," Feye said, eyes squinting into the sunlight as he tried to get a good angle on his phone for his social media followers.

Ah yes, that legendary feline named El Jefe—The Boss—Mr. Savage was obsessed with. I remember reading somewhere that each jaguar had its own specific arrangement of rosette patterns. Like a human fingerprint. El Jefe was supposed to have a heart-shaped one on his right hip and a question mark over the left side of his rib cage.

I whispered that to Feye, who tried to zoom in with his camera to see if he could spot any of those markings. But no luck!

"We just *gotta* get a closer look to see if it's him," Feye said. "Maybe if we climb a tree?"

"We've got this. We are pro climbers," Leo said.

"Leo, you've never climbed a tree in your life," Mónica said quietly, earning her a glare from her brother.

"How hard can it be?" He shrugged and hoisted himself onto the first branch of the tree next to the jaguar's with ease. "Don't make me look bad, Sis." He extended a hand to help her up into the tree with him.

Mónica sighed and took his hand. Together, they climbed higher and higher.

Above the treetops, I spotted a majestic bald eagle riding the air currents. I gasped. This region was the only area in the world where military macaws and bald eagles shared a habitat. The eagle disappeared, and I turned my attention back to the adventure unfolding before my eyes.

"Are you getting this, Feye?" I whispered to my brother, who silently motioned to his Villalobos Vision camera and cell phone camera, which were now both pointing in the direction of the jaguar.

BALD EAGLE

- The bald eagle is a bird of prey native to North America.
- Its main source of food is fish, so it is most often found near large bodies of open water.
- Despite its name, this eagle is not actually bald! The feathers on the top of its head and on its tail are white.

Mónica and Leo whispered to each other as they climbed up the tree. The stealthy cat's ears twitched in their direction even though its eyes were still closed. I had a bad feeling about this.

I was about to tell the twins to come back down, when—

Crack!

My head whipped around just in time to see Leo crash to the ground with a sickening thump. I ran over to my friend as he rolled off a large broken branch onto the ground. He grimaced and gingerly held one of his arms, muttering in obvious pain.

Mónica jumped from the tree, landing in a pile of leaves next to her brother. She looked at us with fear in her eyes.

"It's okay, Leo! It's going to be okay," I reassured him as the initial shock of falling out of the tree wore off and he quieted down.

"Oh man, my arm and shoulder hurt," Leo mumbled, rubbing off some of the dirt that clung to his face.

"Here, let me see," I said. I carefully poured

some of my cool water over Leo's shoulder, brushing away the dirt that clung to the fresh scrapes there. Surprisingly, they didn't look too bad.

"Can you move it?" Feye asked. He sounded more grown-up than usual. Leo shook his head, still clutching his arm. It hadn't even been a few minutes and I could already see some swelling.

I looked up to see if I could spot the jaguar on its branch—it wasn't there. The commotion must have made it escape to someplace quieter. Or . . . it was lurking around, watching us. I pushed the thought out of my mind and tried to focus on Leo.

"I think you've just sprained your shoulder," Feye said, looking around in his backpack for something and frowning when he came up empty-handed. "But I'm not sure about that arm. I wanna make you a sling, but I can't find anything useful in my mini first aid kit. We have antibiotic cream, though."

He handed the tube to me, and I dabbed at the wounds on Leo's shoulder.

"Where did you earn your doctor's degree?"

Leo asked, wincing through the pain. The scrapes weren't bleeding, thankfully, but I didn't want them to get infected.

"We took a first aid course at the zoo," Feye said all matter-of-factly, once again looking through his backpack as if what he needed would magically appear.

"If we don't have bandages or gauze for a sling . . . what are we going to use, Feye?" I asked. Without a sling, would Leo even be able to walk out of the forest to get help?

CHAPTER EIGHT

Rip!

I looked between the concentration on my brother's face and the pain etched in Leo's as Feye continued to tug and rip until the bottom of his T-shirt under his khaki button-down was gone.

"When professional medical help isn't nearby, you can still help—all with a simple T-shirt!" Feye mumbled, the bit of T-shirt still in his mouth and now slightly damp.

Feye continued to tear at the bits of his shirt in his hand, making wide strips and folding them into a length long enough to cover the wound on Leo's shoulder. He handed me the homemade bandages and grabbed tape from his first aid kit. He patiently waited while I lay the strips to cover the oozing scrape. Once in place, he taped the edges so it wouldn't move.

"But what about a sling?" Mónica asked, looking at my brother as if he had just done the coolest thing ever. And to be fair . . . yeah, he had. It's not every day someone literally rips up their clothing for you!

Feye held up a finger to signal "hold on" as he unbuttoned his khaki shirt and completely took off the undershirt he had just torn. We waited as he put the khaki shirt back on, grabbed a safety pin from his backpack, and then came over to Leo. He helped him put the torn shirt on. Then Feye pulled the bottom of it up and over Leo's forearm to make a hammock. Then he pinned the shirt to itself and then to Leo's shirt to keep it in place.

"Wow," I said, impressed at my older brother's quick thinking and creativity.

"That was amazing!" Mónica said.

"Yeah, thanks a lot, man," Leo said, looking down at his arm in awe.

Feye shrugged. "No worries, mate," Feye said with a wink. "But don't thank me just yet. We gotta get you back to camp and get that properly looked at."

We nodded, dusted ourselves off, and looked around. After a few beats of silence, we all realized we had no idea where we were! In the chaos of Leo's getting hurt, we had gotten ourselves utterly lost.

"I don't even know what direction we came from!" wailed Mónica.

"Hey, don't freak out!" Feye said, whipping out his phone from his back pocket. "That's what GPS is for!"

But Feye's phone had no bars. And when the rest of us took out our phones, we all got the same message: no bars, and no way to call the adults.

The sky was no longer a brilliant blue, but a dusty indigo. The sun was starting to dip back down to make way for the night. If I had only looked up at the position of the sun when we started out, maybe I would have known if we were east or west . . . but I hadn't. None of us had.

"It's getting dark," I said.

Mónica was furiously rubbing her arms, which had broken out into goose bumps. Was it the cold or the uneasiness of possibly being lost in the woods? I didn't want to ask.

Then it clicked for me. "It's cold! Yes! I bet our family will have started a fire to keep warm while they're waiting for us to meet them."

If we could see the smoke, then we would be able to figure out where our parents were.

"But how are we ever going to see it through all this?" Feye asked, motioning to the forest around us.

I leaned on a nearby tree. "By climbing a tree, of course."

Feye snorted. "You're kidding, right?" When I didn't say anything, he continued. "I just bandaged one of you up for falling out of a tree! I don't have any other T-shirts to rip up!"

"Technically, I didn't fall," Leo said. "The branch broke and *then* I fell. Don't make it sound like I was uncoordinated or something."

"Or something." Feye laughed.

"Come on, Feye," I said. "Have you ever seen me fall out of a tree? We've climbed bigger ones than this!"

He knew I had a point, as our parents had let us explore nature since before we could walk, gradually building our skills and testing our boundaries. Feye let out a big sigh and turned around.

"Are you . . . ignoring me?" I asked, confused.

"No," he replied. "I'm turning around for deniability—if you fall out of this tree and break every bone in your body, I can tell our parents I had no idea what you were doing and didn't see you."

I couldn't help but laugh. That older sibling logic was foolproof!

"Just do it quickly, okay?" he asked. "Quickly but safely."

I looked at the tree and did a circle around its base, making sure it was strong enough for me to climb. The short walk around didn't show me any branches or roots that could be rotten, and I didn't spy any cracks or splits in the trunk, or large areas where bark was missing.

Mónica squatted near the tree I was standing by and put her hands out as a ledge for me to step on. Then I boosted myself up to the first thick branch. Before shifting my whole weight onto the branch, I put a foot on it and gently pushed it down to see if it was sturdy enough.

"Are you able to get a good grip?" she asked. I nodded, remembering the "three on tree" rule our parents had taught us—always have either two hands and one foot or two feet and one hand in contact with the tree.

That's what I focused on as I slowly made my way up the different branches, checking and exploring every inch of the brown wood before choosing one to climb next.

I really hoped a spider didn't crawl on me . . . or worse, land on me. While I loved and appreciated every animal, spiders were not welcome right now.

"Does that branch feel sturdy?" Leo asked. I looked down to see Feye peeking over his shoulder to see how high I was and then quickly turning back around.

I didn't feel like I was conquering the tree as I made my way up it . . . If anything, I felt respect as I reached the last branch. I was surrounded by the different hues of green treetops. For a moment, I closed my eyes and took a deep breath in. I smelled pure, crisp, clean air. You couldn't get this in the city, that's for sure!

As I opened my eyes, I looked around for signs of our family. Surely, they would have a campfire . . . right?

I had almost finished scanning the horizon without spotting any smoke when I noticed something.

Yes, there it was—a plume of smoke slowly drifting skyward and mixing with the surrounding clouds, not too far away from us. I smiled—success!

Keeping three on the tree, I pulled out my small compass key chain and looked at the direction it was pointing to when I aimed it at the fire: southwest. Perfect. I stuffed it back in my pocket and made my way down to where everyone was waiting at the base. Feye already had open arms, ready to grab me from the bottom branch.

"Did you see them?" he asked when he had thoroughly given me a once-over.

I nodded and pulled out the compass. Standing at the base of the tree I had just climbed, I turned in the direction I saw the fire until the compass once again read southwest.

Pointing forward, I showed them all my compass. "This is the way the compass said the smoke was coming from. If we keep going this direction for about a mile or two, we'll come across them."

"Alright, then," Feye said, slinging his backpack

onto his back and grabbing Leo's for him. "Lead the way, Explorer Adrianna."

Grabbing my own bag and keeping one eye on the compass and one on the forest floor so I didn't trip over any roots or branches, I led us toward what I hoped was our family.

CHAPTER NINE

By the time we emerged from the forest and into the clearing, I spotted a small campfire. The sky had turned a dark navy blue. We had reached it just in time! Being lost in the forest was one thing, being lost in the forest at night . . . That was a recipe for disaster.

Suddenly, I heard my dad's voice.

"There you guys are!" he said in a singsong voice as he spotted us, quickly putting the lid on a cast-iron skillet that was over the fire. He ran to us and before he could hug me or Feye, his eyes went to Leo in his makeshift sling.

"Leo!" Daniela cried out, rushing over to her son

and getting down on her knees to get a better look at his injuries.

"What happened, Feye?" Mom asked, coming over and signaling Dad to go stay with the food so it wouldn't burn.

"He fell out of a tree," Feye began to explain.

"Well, technically, the branch broke. I didn't fall," Leo said.

Feye rolled his eyes. "As I was saying, he fell out of the tree. He's got some scratches on his shoulder that we cleaned up and bandaged. Nothing too deep. The arm itself looks a bit swollen. He might want to go to a doctor for that."

Daniela raised an eyebrow in Feye's direction. I couldn't tell if she was impressed with his assessment of the injuries or annoyed that her kid had fallen out of a tree under his watch. It wasn't exactly a secret that Feye and I had a track record of getting into trouble during filming.

"You did this?" she asked, motioning to the homemade sling and bandages.

Feye looked down at his shoes. "Yeah, sorry I didn't have proper stuff to use. I need to refill my travel first aid kit, it seems."

Daniela stood up and gave him a hug. "Thank you."

"Aw, *no era nada*," Feye said, brushing off the compliment, but I saw that smile on his face.

"Feye, I am really impressed!" Daniela said.

"I'm so glad we got you to take those emergency fieldwork classes!" Mom laughed. Daniela took Leo to her car, where she replaced Feye's rustic bandages and sling with a proper sling and actual Band-Aids.

"I'll be taking you to the local doctor tonight, mister," she told Leo as they rejoined us just as Dad started serving us some hearty soup with bread. As we huddled around the fire for warmth, allowing the soup to warm our insides, the adults talked about their adventures while we ate and quieted our rumbling stomachs.

"The crew and Savage should be back at the house by now, downloading all the shots they got," Mom said, looking at her watch. Apparently, they had left in a hurry, with Mr. Savage saying something about an important meeting in town.

"I really want to know who does business with him here," Daniela remarked as she slurped some of her soup. "His Spanish isn't really the best."

Feye and I exchanged a look.

"We need to look over that footage from the first four camera traps tonight," Dad said as he bit into some buttered bread.

"First, we need to clean up," Mom pointed out. "Then we will make sure Leo gets the medical attention he needs. After that, we'll head back to the house."

Everyone nodded in agreement, and the rest of dinner was eaten in silence as we enjoyed second helpings and even thirds for some people—*ahem*, Dad.

Daniela used the satellite phone to call the local doctor. Mónica, Feye, and I cleaned up the makeshift campsite while our parents packed the car. It wasn't until I had buckled up and leaned my head against the cool window that I realized how exhausted I truly was. My back hurt, and my hands ached from gripping the tree branches so tightly. My legs felt like jelly.

I looked over to see my brother, his eyes already closed and a soft snore escaping his open lips. The twins weren't any better, both also asleep and leaning against each other. I'm not sure when I decided to join them, because the next thing I knew I was jolted awake by Dad pressing the brakes a little too hard and causing my head to smack against the window. *Ouch!*

"Dad!" I complained, rubbing my head.

"Sorry, A," he apologized. "Alright, everyone, we're back!"

Daniela unbuckled herself and came around to help the half-asleep Leo, tucking him into her car and speeding off to the doctor. The rest of us marched inside to download the camera trap footage to analyze.

The house was warm and smelled of freshly made, buttery popcorn. We were welcomed by Alice and Mark, who offered us hot chocolate.

As my parents updated them about what happened to Leo, I snuck into the bathroom to take a quick shower and rinse off the day's sweat and dirt. I refused to come out until my hair was washed and there was no longer forest floor under my fingernails.

"A! Stop hogging all the hot water." Feye pounded on the door. "Your turn to download your camera trap film, anyway."

I sighed and turned the water taps off, breathing in the scent of flowery body wash and steam. Changing into clean filming clothes, I hung up my towel and walked out of the bathroom only to have Feye immediately lock himself in and turn on the shower.

"Anything interesting so far?" I asked Mónica as I sat down next to her and began the downloading process. She was already on a laptop watching her footage, eyes glued to the screen even as she sipped hot cocoa.

"No, nothing yet," she mumbled, entranced.

"She's lying—she just saw a jaguar!" Connor

said from the corner of the room where he was setting up the microphones to capture our reactions
to whatever we saw on the screens. I looked up to
see Mark near him, camera ready to start rolling
whenever. Meanwhile, Alice, who was on the couch
opposite us, had her camera on her lap.

"Hey, that's interesting!" I said to Mónica, who
shrugged and replied, "Not so much when you see
them every day of your life."

"Did it look healthy?" I asked, pressing for more
details.

"Sure did—looked extra fat." Mónica stopped
her film and rewound until a large jaguar filled the
screen. Yup, it looked big . . . really big.

The front door flew open and there stood Leo,
a frown on his face as he held up his arm that was
now in a stark white cast.

We all gasped and his frown deepened.

"Leo! Keep it in the sling, please," his mother chas-
tised from behind him, and he did what he was told.

It turned out Leo had a hairline fracture, and

while he would have gotten away with it just wrapped up in a sling, Daniela insisted on him having a cast on the arm for a few weeks to properly heal.

"Well, it could've been worse, *amigo,*" Feye said, emerging from the bathroom to hear the end of Daniela's explanation.

He wandered past Mónica's screen and stopped in his tracks. "Whoa! Check out the huge cat!"

Daniela crossed the lounge room in a few strides to see what we were looking at, her eyes growing large. She waved over my parents, and the crew sprang into action—they knew something good was about to go down.

"What you are seeing right now is a female we call Marisol, who mated with a male a little while ago . . . and it seems Marisol is pregnant!" Daniela exclaimed.

A pregnant jaguar!

CHAPTER TEN

Daniela called up all the ranchers to let them know about our latest discovery thanks to the camera traps, stressing to them that the jaguar was pregnant and very important. She didn't want anyone to accidentally harm it. It wasn't long after she called Señor José that he knocked on her front door and wanted an explanation as to how more jaguars competing for food—his cattle—was a good thing.

"If you do the things I suggested doing at the last meeting, then it shouldn't be a problem," she reminded him, offering him a cup of warm tea as he settled into a chair in the kitchen. "Since corralling your herd at night and having Jorge drop off those water buffalo at your place, have you had much of a problem?"

He took his time drinking his tea, pondering her question. He finally shook his head. "No," he said.

"That's the science working, Señor José," she replied with a wink. He chuckled and continued sipping his tea as Daniela explained that she would be setting up some more snares near his house to catch jaguars lurking there.

"What will you do with them?" the old man asked, intrigued.

"She's going to tag them!" I replied, joining him at the kitchen table with my own cup of tea. Mónica sat beside me.

Daniela started explaining to him what the snares looked like, how quickly everyone would respond to a trapped jaguar, and what the satellite collars would tell scientists about the jaguar's movements.

"Would I be told if a jaguar has been caught on my land?" he asked.

Daniela nodded. "Immediately, and we might even suggest rounding up your cattle after we release it . . . just in case," she said.

Señor José once again nodded, finished his tea, and thanked us all for our time. As Daniela walked him to the front door, I could hear her saying that we would all be going out into the field tomorrow to put a few more camera traps up.

"Is it true, *Mami*?" I asked my mom, who looked up from her TV show notes to nod and give me a big smile. "And we have a special guest joining us, too."

I really, really hoped that meant some sort of celebrity . . . maybe Sofía Vergara?

Leo quickly dashed my hopes with a clap of his hands and a big grin of his own. "Myko!"

"Who?" Feye asked, taking his headphones off to finally listen in on the conversation happening around him.

"Our dog," Mónica explained, scrolling through her cell phone until she found what she was looking for. At first glance, the dog in the photo resembled a German shepherd with its rich, mahogany-colored fur and black ears, but Leo explained it was a dog breed known as Belgian Malinois.

"Myko is a very smart and obedient dog. Mom's trained him to detect the scent of jaguars," Mónica said as she scrolled through more photos of Myko as both a puppy and an older dog.

"He also has strong protective and territorial instincts," Leo said. "That's why he hasn't been here . . . Mr. Jorge is bringing him over soon."

A bark outside alerted us to the fact that "soon" actually meant "now."

Myko bounded through the front door and tore into the living room. As Mónica and Leo opened up their arms to cuddle their beloved dog, he quickly surveyed us all, his dark eyes piercing through us. His wagging tail told me we had passed his quick inspection.

Myko ended up sleeping near the front door,

barking when Mr. Savage eventually walked in. Mr. Savage told us our start time of seven in the morning, before walking into his room and shutting off all the lights.

I wondered where he had been. But it was getting late. I headed off to get my rest. I'd need it if tomorrow was anything like today!

The next morning after breakfast, we all headed back into the reserve. We jogged behind Myko. He had his nose glued to the hot forest floor and was practically sprinting toward what we hoped would be a jaguar.

"Like his close relatives from the same lines, Myko has a great nose, can handle heat, and is both trainable and intelligent," Daniela said into the camera that was following us. We continued to pick up the pace and follow Myko on his journey to find us any clues of the wild cats nearby. "He has been trained to bark when he finds jaguar scat, or poop."

"So that means he can distinguish it from the scat of other large cats?" Dad asked, a little out of breath.

Daniela nodded, explaining that Myko was also trained to bark when he found ocelot scat. She sometimes traveled with him to parts of the United States to help out with ocelot projects there.

"He's stopping, *Mami*!" Leo said. Myko slowed down and started barking as we came to a wall of rocks and a steep drop beyond them. His whole body seemed to point at a pile of poop that was under a thick patch of plants near the imposing wall. Daniela took out some dog treats from a plastic pouch in her pocket and gave them to Myko as he panted with delight after a job well done.

"It's smelly, so it must mean it's fresh!" I said, burying my nose in my T-shirt. Connor gave me a look, and I knew I had rubbed the microphone on my shirt the wrong way. Maybe it was for the best that my comment wouldn't be used on TV. Out of the corner of my eye, I could see Alice getting closer to the scat, her camera lens practically touching the steamy pile.

"Perfect place to put some cameras, then," Daniela said, taking one out and looking around to see where she would put it.

"That cleft in the rocks seems like a good hiding place for a big cat," Mom commented. Mark's camera focused in on her and then at what she was pointing at.

"Talk about it being a place of refuge, Evelyn," Mr. Savage said. He was bright red all over and completely out of breath.

"Right . . . so in the wild, jaguar mothers try to find a suitable den—such as an underground burrow, the space under a thick patch of plants, or a cleft in the rocks like this one—to give birth," Mom said. "If we're lucky, maybe we might see the one we recently captured on camera give birth here!"

As Mom narrated this with Mark's camera pointed at her, Alice's camera focused on Daniela, who was making sure the camera trap she was setting up was securely fastened on a nearby tree and pointing right at the rock wall.

"There!" she said with a satisfied grin. We all gave her a thumbs-up.

A loud tinkling noise broke through the quietness of the forest and Mr. Savage let out a frustrated groan.

"Cut, *cut*! Whose phone is that?" Mr. Savage demanded. We all looked at one another and then realized it was Daniela's.

"Sorry, one moment," she said as she fumbled to get the phone out of her deep cargo shorts pocket. Alice's camera never wavered off Daniela's face as she answered her cell phone and listened intently to whoever was talking to her. A smile spread across her face and she thanked the caller.

"Señor José just called to say one of the snares caught a jaguar! My team just called him and—" she started to say, but her phone started ringing again. "That's them!"

"Perfect! A jaguar to tag!" Mr. Savage clapped.

"Let's go. Walk and talk, Daniela, we gotta get to this kitty as fast as possible."

As we jogged back the way we had come, Mr. Savage started giving orders to the camera crew on what angles he wanted to capture, what camera lenses they should use, and that Feye and I should be the ones to tag this cat.

Zooming back toward town, I was grateful that the cars were all-terrain as they veered off the paved road and onto dirt paths toward the GPS location that Daniela's team had given her. A large group of volunteers waved us down and had us park a safe distance away from the big cat that had been tranquilized a few minutes before.

"How are its vitals?" Daniela asked, ignoring the cameras now trained on her. I tried to keep up with everyone as we made our way closer to the knocked-out jaguar.

Out of the corner of my eye, I was surprised to see Señor José there, watching everyone as they moved efficiently to take the necessary measurements of the cat. I gave him a small wave and he returned it.

"She's good, all levels are good," a volunteer with brown hair and bright blue eyes said, handing Daniela a chart with notes scribbled all over it. After scanning the document, Daniela smiled brightly and looked at me.

"Want to tag a jaguar?" she asked.

"*¡Sí!*" I shouted, unable to keep my excitement in. The same volunteer produced a thick collar similar to the one we had seen before, except this one was black.

As we got closer to the jaguar, I looked up to Feye and Daniela and asked, "Can we invite Señor José to help?" All three of us turned to look at the older gentleman, who was still on the outskirts of the organized chaos that was this scientific TV production.

"I think that is a wonderful idea, Adrianna," Daniela said.

She walked over to Señor José and explained to him what I had proposed.

"That was a nice thing you did, A," Mom murmured from behind me.

Señor José returned with Daniela and followed her instructions on where to kneel down by the jaguar. Feye and I sat on either side of him and listened to Daniela as she explained the science behind the tags in a little bit more detail for Señor José.

"What do you want to name her?" Daniela whispered to us.

"Can we name her Esperanza?" I looked at Señor José as I said this. "It means hope . . . and I know everyone here has hope for the future of jaguar conservation both in this town and beyond."

Señor José leaned over and stroked Esperanza's fur softly, helping Feye and me maneuver the collar around her neck. We let him do the honor of clipping the two sides together.

For the longest time, Señor José didn't say anything. He stroked Esperanza's fur, looked at the scientific tech around her neck, and eventually met our eyes.

"Everyone, including me," he whispered.

I quietly ran my hand along Esperanza's fur and flashed a small smile at Señor José.

CHAPTER ELEVEN

The next day was a busy one. Mom and Dad spent the day with Mark and Mr. Savage scouring the woods for the injured jaguar and the pregnant female. Feye and I were stuck with Alice and Connor, sticking camera traps around the woods. The work was boring and hot, but would hopefully pay off with at least one jaguar to tag.

In the evening after dinner, we all sat in the lounge room polishing up cameras, downloading footage from camera USBs to a hard drive, or passing around cups of steaming tea to those who asked for them.

Daniela's phone beeped and she looked down.

Whatever she read there made her scrunch up her face. "Huh, weird," she muttered.

"What's going on, *amiga*?" Mom asked. Daniela motioned her to come closer and take a look at the screen.

I was curious and inched myself closer to my mom. I caught Feye looking at me with an eyebrow raised. He pointed to his mouth and nose and smiled.

Stop having a "sticky beak." *Right.*

I pouted, mad that Connor had taught Feye that Australian phrase for being nosy, and sat back down in my chair. That earned a smirk from Feye, to which I replied with an eye roll.

Not even a second after I sat back down did Mom and Daniela dash off to the other side of the room to grab a laptop and hook it up to the television.

"What's happening?" Leo asked as they fiddled with the connections.

"I've got alerts set up on my phone for certain

cameras that jaguars regularly pass by," Daniela explained, holding up her phone, which was constantly vibrating with text message alerts. "Thanks to the motion detectors there, this camera is letting us know something is hanging around, and I'm kind of keen to watch!"

"Let us see!" I shouted.

We huddled around the large screen, and after a few more minutes of my mom and Daniela trying to link the two devices, the TV and computer finally synced up to show a live feed of a huge female jaguar.

"She's a bit fat," Feye joked, earning a side-eye from Dad.

"She's not fat, Feye! She's pregnant!" Mónica said, her eyes wide and glued to the visibly pregnant female.

We had caught our pregnant jaguar on camera once again! Everyone cheered, some clapping, others shushing even though there was no noise coming from the computer or television.

"What is she doing?" I asked, staring at the screen with my head sideways. It looked like she was sitting down, not finding the position comfortable, and doing a turn before sitting down once more and repeating the whole thing all over again.

"Is she constipated?" Feye asked. Leo let out a laugh. I couldn't tell if my brother was being serious or not.

"Can jaguars get constipated?" Feye asked again. "I'm serious! It looks like she's trying to poop but can't."

"No, silly!" Mónica teased, one of her slender fingers pointing out the round tummy of the jaguar. "It isn't trying to poop. I think we're about to see a baby jaguar!"

She said it so calmly that it took a second for the reality of what was happening to sink in.

"Mark! Alice!" Mr. Savage barked, his eyes wide as he fully understood what we were watching. "Get the cameras!"

The camera crew dashed around in different

directions. In the blink of an eye, they were back and ready to record us watching the mother jaguar give birth.

"Can you guys tell me a little bit more about jaguars?" Mr. Savage said, trying to get us to fill in the silent moments.

Mom pushed back her hair and, without looking away said, "Jaguars have no defined breeding season and will mate any time of year. Their pregnancy lasts about one hundred days."

I jumped in at her pause. "And they typically give birth to two to four cubs!"

The camera feed wasn't the best quality, but we could see the mother jaguar was panting and struggling to get her first cub to make its grand entrance.

"Come on, *mamá*! You can do it!" I cheered her on, even though I knew she wouldn't be able to hear me.

I tried to ignore the fuzzy microphone above our heads that came closer to me, and the bright red light of the camera pointed at us. This was history we were witnessing!

Suddenly, Mom gasped and pointed at the screen as a little blob plopped onto the earth. The mother turned quickly to lick her new baby clean. I couldn't believe we had just seen a new life be born!

Shaking my head, I turned my attention back to the monitor. This memory would live forever in my head, I just knew it.

"Can you believe it?!" Leo whispered.

I broke out in a smile. No, I couldn't believe it. And as we were all excitedly talking among ourselves, another little cub slid out of the mother jaguar—a new animal soul that would call this forest home.

CHAPTER TWELVE

Daniela let her volunteers know what was happening and instructed a few to guard the cats overnight from a safe distance. When we woke up the next morning, we had more exciting news: We had jaguars ready to tag! It wasn't the injured jaguar but it was apparently a huge male.

We all got ready quickly and ate breakfast on the way over to the site. Once on location, we followed Daniela to where the sedated jaguar was lying.

Soon, cameras were rolling, and my parents were in educator mode. "The jaguar is the largest wild cat in the Western Hemisphere, existing in eighteen countries in Latin America, from Mexico to Argentina," Dad narrated into the camera as he got a collar from out of a nearby box and made his way toward the sleeping giant. "Unfortunately, these big cats have been erased from forty percent of their historic range—they are actually already extinct in Uruguay and El Salvador!"

Dad knelt and attached the collar around the neck of the large male, making just a slight dent in the thick fur. "We don't know how many of these creatures are left in the wild, so scientific tools such as camera traps"—he paused and pointed at the cameras around us—"and these collars are vital in making sure we learn as much as possible about the ones that remain, like Jorge here. That way we can better protect them from the various threats they face!"

Mr. Savage blew a chef's kiss into the air, turning to face us and saying that that's how it was done. Dad blushed from the compliment, not used to getting it from our usually grumpy producer. He sure was in a good mood today.

"Do you hear that?" Dad asked, putting his hand

around one ear as he stood up from beside the jaguar. Over the regular chatter of the forest, I could make out the faint sound of something being sawed.

"Is someone cutting down a tree?!" I asked.

Feye shook his head. "No . . . that's a jaguar's roar!"

Whoa! I barely had a moment to fully appreciate that cool fact when Daniela announced we had our second jaguar of the day—maybe it was the one we had just heard roaring.

"It's a possibility," she said as we climbed into the van and headed toward the direction of the roar, leaving behind some of her team to monitor the big cat until it woke up. When we got there, Daniela's team was already there making sure the cat was comfortable after it had slowly fallen on its side thanks to the tranquilizer dart.

"Evelyn, get in there and do your thing!" Mr. Savage said as Mom and Daniela headed toward the jaguar and began taking measurements and calling out its vitals.

"The threats to jaguars here are many, including

deforestation, illegal tree logging, road construction and its associated impacts, including habitat loss, and overhunting," Mom said to a nearby camera as she clipped the collar around the resting cat's neck. She had named the young female Rosita. "There is also quite a lot of frustration and hatred toward the jaguars that kill local livestock. It's our hope that working with local scientists, we can elevate appreciation for these animals through future educational resources and community outreach!"

Mr. Savage gave Mom a thumbs-up sign and said something to Mark that I couldn't quite make out, but he shifted his position to get another angle of Mom. Daniela swooped in to double-check that the collar on Rosita was good to go and radioed her team to keep an eye on the jaguar through the cameras.

"We have another one in a snare not too far away from here that my team is sedating right now, so if we want to film it, we need to go," Daniela told Mr. Savage, loud enough for all of us to hear. "Now, come on!"

Three jaguars?! No way!

"Aren't jaguars typically loners? Why are they all so close to one another?" I asked my mom. She was about to answer when Mr. Savage barged in.

"Feye, tell us about why this science stuff is so important," Mr. Savage suggested, motioning to the collar and Daniela.

"Scientists like Daniela play a critical role in providing scientific data to guide and support the development of a recovery plan for these cats," Feye said, looking at Mark's camera, which was closest to his face, while Alice's was zooming in on the collar around the knocked-out cat. "They've used camera traps to evaluate jaguar numbers here and the effectiveness of the tools they've implemented for conflict reduction. But these collars add another layer to the whole story."

I wouldn't have believed we had captured a third jaguar if I was not standing behind the cameras as Daniela and Feye worked on the male (which Feye had named Godzilla), while the footage captured it all.

"Awesome, cut, Feye. Adrianna, it's going to be your turn last," Mr. Savage instructed as he looked at his field notebook and jotted something down, his pencil flying across the page.

How was Mr. Savage so confident we would be finding another jaguar to tag? We already had three in just a few hours! Surely, that had to be a record somewhere . . . Surely, there weren't any left.

Daniela's ringing phone said otherwise. As she talked on the phone, she pointed to the van, letting us know a fourth jaguar had been captured and we had to get to it *pronto*!

Once more we dashed toward the car and flew across the muddy terrain to get to our prize: a small female that I would get to name and tag. I could hardly contain my excitement as I was being mic'd up, watching as my parents and Daniela took all sorts of samples from the jaguar.

Dad had just finished taking some paw measurements when I was given the okay by Connor to join them. Alice and Mark hauled the cameras up to their shoulders to film me as I was handed the heavy satellite tracking collar to put around the animal that was now just a few inches away.

I buried my fingers into her soft fur, in awe of how clean it was for something that lived entirely outside. "Into the camera, Adrianna," Mr. Savage reminded me, and I looked up at Alice and smiled.

"For me, jaguars are the perfect example of mysterious beauty. We still have so many questions about the jaguars here, and these GPS collars will hopefully give us some answers," I said, holding up the two-pound collar. I pointed out the two small antennas on top and the aluminum enclosure for the battery and transmitter on the bottom. "It will send out a radio signal to a satellite system that scientists like Daniela use to track the jaguars from just about anywhere. The batteries can last up to two years, and don't worry—they don't hurt the jaguars."

I knew that scientists frequently used radio collars for studying wild animals, but I had never held one like this before. As I snapped it around the neck of the jaguar, her name suddenly came to me thanks to her yellow fur. "By protecting jaguars, like Honey here, and the places where they live, we're also helping to look after other wildlife."

"Perfect!" Mr. Savage beamed, his finger circling in the air—his way of saying to wrap things up.

"Hold on, sorry, everyone. We might need to retake that; the camera is acting up," Alice said, getting up from the forest floor and turning her camera upside down. "Mark, can you get this angle, please, while I figure this out?"

"What's the holdup, Alice?" Mr. Savage bellowed, his voice laced with impatience.

"Sorry, boss—let me just grab a replacement piece," she said, and jogged over to her bag that held all her camera supplies. She rummaged around it for a little bit before letting out a frustrated sigh.

"Ah, shoot!" Alice muttered, a displeased look on her face. "I thought I had packed more of those dang things." After typing on her phone for a few seconds, she let out a groan and announced the only place to get what she needed was in a town a few hours north.

"Where up north?" Daniela asked, coming closer to look over Alice's shoulder to see the map. She smiled.

"How would you all like a change of scenery tomorrow?" Daniela proposed. "I know something that will be worth your while."

CHAPTER THIRTEEN

The next morning, I rolled down the van window, breathing in the salty air of Mexico's Baja Peninsula. The Gulf of California was legendary. The famous ocean explorer Jacques Cousteau once called it "the world's aquarium." It was home to an astounding number of sea creatures, many of them endemic and found nowhere else on the planet! I looked down at my lap to finish scribbling the last of what I knew about the gulf into my field notebook.

GULF OF CALIFORNIA

- *Also known as the Sea of Cortés (Sea of Cortez) or Vermilion Sea.*
- *Over 700 miles long!*

• *John Steinbeck wrote a book about his voyage here aboard a scientific collecting expedition in 1940.*

"Working again?" Feye teased. He held his phone up in the air, taking selfies with the shimmering blue water zipping past in the background.

"This isn't a break, Feye." I smiled. "We are technically still filming."

After a semi-successful field excursion, Mr. Savage had discovered that Daniela's husband, Manolo, was a marine biologist who studied the critically endangered vaquita, a porpoise whose numbers had diminished drastically over the last couple of decades. He said he thought it would make a good "change of environment" for the show and wanted to film us swimming around the kelp forests, marveling at the fish.

Really, we all knew it was Daniela's idea to go visit him because he was near the town that had Alice's missing camera part. And after a quick pit stop to grab it, we were on our way!

I flipped the page in my field notebook and started writing down an entry for the vaquita since, apparently, there were only a handful of these creatures left.

"*Basta*, enough writing and enjoy the view, little sis!" My older brother snatched my notebook out of my hands and pointed to our view.

"This is one of the most biologically diverse bodies of water on earth," said Mom.

"It was formed four to five million years ago, thanks to a tectonic rift between Baja California and the North American Plate, making it one of the world's youngest seas," Dad said, finishing her sentence perfectly.

I snapped a pic and sent it to Alessi. I wished she were here to see it in person!

But for all its beauty, it made my heart sink a little knowing that the Gulf of California was an ecosystem in decline. Decades of overfishing had unbalanced this beautiful habitat, taking top predators such as sharks and marlins out of the food chain and

VAQUITA

- A species of porpoise found only in the northern end of the Gulf of California in Baja California, Mexico.
- It is the smallest of all living cetaceans.
- They are critically endangered, with fewer than 10 individuals left!

leading to a rise in other species that was throwing food webs out of balance. Dad once talked about seeing hundreds of hammerhead sharks at local dive sites here in the seventies . . . Today, I knew a sighting like that would be rare because fishing here had dramatically reduced their population numbers.

I closed my eyes and once again took in the briny air. Soon we would be dipping into the cold water, and I hoped I'd see some sharks in between the rocks and kelp. And as we turned left, I couldn't help but notice the rich sea was a stark contrast to the forbidding desert at its edge. We were headed to a blue oasis, but all around us was oppressive heat and an endless mix of beige, brown, yellow, and orange sand and dirt. The van slowed as we neared a bronze statue of Cousteau clutching a diving mask and staring out to sea.

"Hello, one of Adrianna's heroes!" Dad chuckled, making a grand show of waving at the statue before continuing along to meet Leo and Mónica's dad. All our heads were now hanging out the windows as we passed statues of other animals regularly found here: manta rays, sea lions, whales and dolphins, even a giant clam that had a gleaming pearl nestled in its center.

I looked back to see Leo's and Mónica's heads out the window in the car ahead of us. With a final tap of the brakes, we were here! Leo and Mónica flew from their car to a weathered tent where a man who looked like an older version of Leo awaited with open arms.

"Look at you both! It's like you've grown in the last few weeks since I've seen you," he said, kissing each of them. Mónica complained that his thick black mustache was too tickly. Daniela went up to her husband and gave him a smooch, joking that she personally liked the mustache. After the family got a big group hug in, they came over to us and introduced Mr. Manolo and the surrounding area.

Mr. Savage looked small compared to the hulking Mr. Manolo. The two men shook hands and went over some camera specifics about what Mr. Savage would like to film. The list seemed endless, but Mr. Manolo was patient and nodded at every request, even giving tips on the best places to put the cameras for some good angles.

With the business talk out of the way, Mr. Manolo warned us not to pick up anything without checking with him, explaining that Baja was home to many venomous animals like scorpions and snakes. "Make sure to also shake anything before you put it on. Things have a nasty habit of hiding in sleeves and pant legs," he instructed, and we all nodded.

I turned my head up to the unforgiving sun, looking around to see if I could spot some wildlife in this arid wilderness. Outside of some birds, like the vulture-like crested caracaras that lazily soared ahead of us, or the bright vermilion flycatchers near some enticing-looking plants, I couldn't see anything right away. But I knew that once I really started to look, there would be an abundance of wildlife surrounding us.

"While my wife and I prepare quesadillas for lunch, why don't you all go for a quick snorkel off the shore?" Mr. Manolo said, holding up a weathered iron pan that had probably seen too many field trips. "Leo, with that cast you aren't going into that water, but maybe you and Mónica can help us cook?" The twins looked unhappy, but they nodded and made their way toward the makeshift cooking station that was already being set up.

Feye and I dashed back to the van to change into our wet suits and don our dive booties. We were standing at the edge of the water in less than two minutes flat. As our parents applied sunscreen to our faces, Mr. Manolo pointed out a distant spray of water and called out a variety of culprits responsible for the splash: yellowfin tuna, marlins, maybe even a manta!

"Well, I wouldn't mind catching a manta on camera," Mark said beside us, also in his wet suit and ready to dive under the waves as much as we were.

"Stick together, please," Mom said as we exchanged cheek kisses.

Mom and Dad slipped into the water with Alice behind them, while Mark followed us as we darted underwater, making fish frantically zip about. Even though I was zipped into a thick wet suit, the cold water seeped in and sent a shiver down my spine. The temperature difference was caused by upwelling, where water from the deep ocean was forced upward. It brought nutrients from the depths to mix with the oxygen-rich surface water.

This cold water, despite being kind of uncomfortable for me, was the whole reason why this area was so full of life! Starfish, crabs, and fish swarmed around me. I could even make out the chatter of dolphins. Kicking my feet, I made a break for the surface to try to spot them above the water.

I pointed my finger above the waves to signal to Mark to look behind him. A large school of common dolphins gathered, seeming to be on the hunt for some unseen prey.

"Alright, Adrianna, you know what to do!" Mark directed, letting me know it was my turn to narrate the scene before me. His camera was half in the water, probably to get both the dolphins below and above the water.

"We are so lucky to be here at the Sea of Cortés, where nearby we are witnessing some beautiful dolphins on the hunt!" I motioned to the chaos behind me. "These are common dolphins, which are seen throughout tropical and temperate waters. They are easily recognizable by their striking crisscross pattern that has, like, a yellowish or tan patch in the middle. Can you see it?"

The dolphins responded to my narrating by porpoising at the water surface, breaching with thrilling clicks and noises that disappeared as soon as they dove back into the ocean.

I looked below to see where my brother was, as I

hadn't seen him come up for air yet. Feye was better at holding his breath than me, but even he needed to breathe! Spotting him, I waved at him to get his attention and saw bubbles erupt from his snorkel like confetti as he kicked up toward the surface.

"There are sea lions here, too!" Feye said, taking in big gulps of air as a dark shadow circled at his feet. I once again put my head underwater to see a little sea lion nibbling at Feye's feet.

Feye quickly interrupted me, though, grabbing the back of my wet suit and hauling me back up to see the dolphins flying across the waves of the water not too far away from us. Like acrobats, they were jumping, flipping, and standing on their tails as they purposefully herded a shoal of silverfish we could now see below us.

"Kids, it's been thirty minutes and I think I can see lunch being set up. Why don't you head on back so you don't accidentally get smacked in the face with a fin or tail!" Mark said, positioning himself so

COMMON DOLPHIN

- Dolphins are mammals, just like humans. They are warm-blooded, breathe air, and give birth to live young.

- There are about six million common dolphins in the world, making them the most widely found members of the cetacean species.

- A fully grown adult common dolphin can be up to eight feet long.

he was between us and the dolphins. "I'll just be a few more minutes."

We didn't need to be told twice! Taking a big breath, we dove underwater and flew through the kelp and rocks before a fun-loving sea lion greeted us, blowing bubbles underwater to warn us off from swimming too close to its lair. As we got closer to the campsite and were finally able to put our feet on the ground, I turned back to see the glittering surface of the deep blue sea. Encounters like this always brought me a sense of privilege: I just got to experience something many people could only dream of doing.

Feye handed me a towel that had been warmed by the sun, and we went back to the camp to devour our quesadillas with the rest of our family and friends. We told Leo and Mónica all about our adventures in the water. Leo then acted out a whole skit of when Mónica had been frightened by a giant whale shark they had once swum with.

"It was really big!" Mónica protested. "And very well camouflaged."

"Sure it was, *hermana*." Leo winked, and we all laughed.

We told them about our most recent run-in with a whale shark in Sri Lanka. The locals we had been swimming with had also been surprised by the massive size of this gentle giant.

With lunch now digesting in our stomachs, Feye and I begged our parents to let us go back out. I pointed to our wet suits that were hanging up to dry on top of a nearby bush and said, "I'm sure they are fully dry by now in this heat!"

"Alright, go ahead," my mom said. Dad reminded us to reapply our sunscreen.

Feye and I high-fived and jogged over to our suits. We shook them out like Mr. Manolo had instructed us to do, before painstakingly trying to squish ourselves back into them.

"Okay . . . so maybe they are still *a little* damp," I joked with Feye as we both jumped up and down, trying to get our butts to squeeze in.

"I win!" Feye triumphantly said as he started to

slip his arms into the top part of the suit just as I stuck a hand in to do the same.

I was met with a jolt of instantaneous and extreme pain. *Ouch!*

When I brought my hand back out, I could see it throbbing slightly and turning reddish near the webbing between my thumb and pointer finger. I rubbed the sore spot to see if I could make the pain go away, but it only made me flinch.

"What's the matter, A?" Feye asked, concern flashing across his face.

"Nothing!" I laughed. "I think I must've run into a jellyfish stinger when diving, and it might've gotten stuck to my suit."

"Leave it to you to get stung by a jellyfish and not even be in the water," he chuckled, rolling his eyes. He reached over to hand me my gloves. "Put these on so you don't get stung again. You've been zapped by their tentacles before; the pain will go away soon enough."

I wasn't sure . . . This pain felt different.

"Something isn't right," I said. I looked down at my tingling hand once more. It was now a bit more swollen and had a single raised dot on it.

"That's . . . not a jellyfish stinger," Feye said. I looked in my wet suit for a loose thorn or something sharp I might have pricked myself with, while Feye looked around our feet.

"A," Feye said, pointing down near our feet. "Look!"

Scurrying away from us was a small scorpion.

"What's up, you two?" Dad asked, but Feye just mutely pointed at the scorpion while I held my hand.

"Oh boy," Mom said while our dad called out for Mr. Manolo. I hoped he would see the scorpion, say it was no big deal, and let me go back into the water. I was already in the suit! And it had taken ages to get into it!

Feye quickly explained what had happened and Mr. Manolo bent down to look at the scorpion before asking us to move away from it.

"Well, Adrianna, seems you just had a run-in with the bark scorpion!" Mr. Manolo said in a calm voice. He bent down so we were both at eye level. "It's common to the Sonoran Desert, and unfortunately it is the most venomous scorpion in North America. So, we need to get you some antivenom right away. But you're going to be okay."

"Feye, can you run over and get the antivenom from the van, please?" Mom asked, her voice shaking a little. She gingerly helped me out of the wet suit I had just taken forever to get into. I knew what antivenom was—medicine that stops venom from binding to tissue and causing serious blood, tissue, or nervous system problems. But I never thought I would need to take it. I had once seen a snake handler at the zoo inject herself with it, but it didn't seem like a lot of fun. Especially for someone who was afraid of needles, like I was.

With a nod, Feye took off.

"It's going to be alright, *mi hija*," Dad reassured me, giving me a kiss on the cheek. "These things happen. That's why we are always prepared and bring the first aid kit!"

BARK SCORPION

- This scorpion is small and light brown in color.
- It is native to the Sonoran Desert region in northwestern Mexico and the southwestern United States.
- They can live for up to seven years.

From the corner of my eye, I could see the bright-green first aid kit propped under one of Feye's arms as he jogged from the van to where we were near the shore. My hand was still throbbing, and I was glad I'd be getting some relief from the antivenom soon enough.

Feye plopped down on the ground and opened up the first aid kit, rummaging through its contents and zipping open a small black bag before letting out a small gasp.

"What is it, *mi amor*?" Mom asked, reaching her hands out for the medical box. But before she could grab hold of it, Feye turned it around to show us the empty pouch where there should have been the antivenom.

CHAPTER FOURTEEN

Have you ever had your arm or leg fall asleep, where it felt like the whole thing was just painful static that you couldn't seem to shake away? Well, that's how my arm felt when I woke up from the nap I was taking in the van when my dad hit a pothole and jolted me out of sleep.

My arm hit the side of the van and I let out a pained cry, cradling my arm. I didn't even remember falling asleep.

I looked out the window to see if I could recognize where we were. I knew we were heading back toward the main road to find a hospital. Apparently, Mr. Manolo's first aid kit had been taken by one of his crew, who was offshore and wouldn't come back until late tonight. We all agreed the best course of action was to get a doctor to check me out as fast as possible.

"Sorry, guys," Dad said, his dark eyes looking at us through the rearview mirror. "The road isn't as paved over here, so things are going to get a bit shaky."

He noticed I was awake, and asked how I was feeling. Shooting pain was making its way up my arm, and the static feeling was almost too unbearable to properly stretch it out. It took some effort, but I was able to straighten the arm. I tried to uncurl and curl my fingers to see how that felt, only to find that I couldn't.

"I . . . I can't move my fingers, you guys," I said, trying not to panic. I knew that it was best to stay calm during situations like this. I tried again, and this time only my pinky finger twitched, while the rest remained outstretched and numb.

"Paralysis, Julio," Mom said from up front. "We need to get her seen, now."

Paralysis was the inability to move or feel part of the body, and while I had seen venom do that to other animals before they were eaten, I had never thought it would happen to me.

"Can I have something for the pain, please?" I asked, hating the slight waver in my voice.

Feye must have seen the look on my face because he leaned over and whispered, "It's okay to be scared. You don't have to be strong all the time . . ."

He took my good hand in his and gave it a squeeze.

I gave him a weak smile. In the front seat, Mr. Savage was telling Dad to turn right up ahead. Earlier, he had been on the phone with a local doctor Mr. Manolo had suggested and was now acting as our GPS—annoying voice and all.

Finally, we could see a small doctor's office up ahead. We parked, and we made our way inside.

The office had stark white walls but thankfully had many brightly colored paintings that made the place look less clinical. Mariachi music played from an old radio in the reception waiting room. When Mr. Savage told the receptionist who we were, she asked us to follow her down the hallway.

The camera crew and Mr. Savage stayed behind with Feye while my parents put a steady hand on each of my shoulders and led me to a bright pink room where a plump doctor with short, curly black hair and caramel-colored eyes greeted us.

"*Hola*, I'm *Doctora* Cruz, and you must be the *familia* Villalobos!" she said brightly, putting on her white doctor's coat and then patting the bed for me to sit on. "And you must be Adrianna; it's so nice to meet you. Do I have your permission to examine your hand?"

I nodded and she let me know it would probably hurt a little as she gently took it in hers. After a few seconds of looking at one side of it, she turned it over.

She poked and prodded a little, asking what had happened. Then she had me describe the different sensations I was feeling and try to move my fingers, once more with no success. She wrote everything down with a blue pen that matched the glasses perched at the end of her nose.

"Well, unfortunately there isn't anything I can do for the paralysis," she said after giving me a shot of antivenom. "But it should go away in the next few days or weeks."

"How did the paralysis even happen?" I asked, curious how such a tiny creature could impact something as big as a human.

She sat down on a rolling chair and scooted across the room to grab a 3D model of an arm to show us. "These purple bits you see here? Those are muscles. And the muscles in your body are controlled by the movement of molecules called ions, which enter muscle cells through special channels that let only certain molecules or atoms pass."

I nodded, letting her know that made sense.

"Now, depending on the type of ion, the muscle will either relax or contract. One such ion is chloride, which helps muscle cells know when to relax.

Scorpion venom contains a very small protein chain called chlorotoxin, and it can block chloride channels and stop chloride ions from entering muscle cells," Doctora Cruz continued. "Without these ions sending signals telling your cells to relax, the muscles in your body all flex at once and that's when paralysis happens."

"So we can't do anything for the paralysis . . . but what about the pain?" I asked, wincing. It still felt like lightning was shooting up my arm every few minutes.

"That I can help with." She winked and stood up, putting down the model of the arm and grabbing a bottle that rattled with pills.

"Take one in the morning and one at night . . . That should help considerably," she said, handing the bottle to Mom.

"*Gracias*, Doctora Cruz," Dad said, shaking her hand.

I peeled myself off the leathery bed and stood up to ask one more question. "Uh, since there's nothing to be done about the pins-and-needles feeling, or the paralysis, but wait . . . can I still do stuff?"

Doctora Cruz gave me a knowing smile. "Do you mean can you still help out with filming? Sure!" She then turned to my parents and added, "It'll actually be good for her to not focus on the pain."

I did a fist bump in the air (with my left hand). Success!

We thanked the doctor once more and left the room to meet the others outside, but the camera crew was nowhere to be seen and Mr. Savage and Feye were pacing back and forth among the chairs.

"There they are!" Feye yelped, running up to us to hear how everything went.

Or at least, that's what I thought, but as soon as he was closer and Dad opened his mouth to speak, Feye interrupted with his own announcement.

"We need to go back to the town *right now*. A jaguar is in trouble!" Feye said.

"Another one?" I asked, looking at Mr. Savage. We all turned our attention to him as he explained that Daniela was already on her way back because she had gotten a call from the rancheros that a jaguar had been cat-napped.

"But how do the rancheros know?" Mom asked, looking confused.

"The camera traps captured it all. Some of the rancheros are helping Daniela's team go through the footage and one of them spotted something funny," Feye said, looking at Mr. Savage to complete the story. He sighed and held out his cell phone. He double-tapped the screen, bringing to life a black-and-white video. If I hadn't watched it on video, I don't know if I would have believed my eyes.

At first there was nothing except a pile of what must have been meat (bait) off to the right side of the camera. Whoever set this up hadn't positioned it well in front of the camera ... unless they didn't know there was a camera. After a few seconds of staring at the meat pile, a gorgeous jaguar came into view, sniffing the air cautiously before gingerly approaching the meat. Suddenly, a spring-loaded platform between two of the surrounding trees was triggered when the jaguar stepped on it and a flexible loop tightened around one of the jaguar's legs.

I looked up at my family, perplexed. That didn't look like a trap Daniela and her team would put down.

Something was wrong.

"Did we put that trap down?" I asked.

Everyone shook their heads.

"The rancheros?" I asked again.

Feye shook his head. The camera feed cut to black.

"When the rancheros went to check this site out, the camera had been covered with paint and the whole snare was missing, along with the jaguar," Feye explained.

CHAPTER FIFTEEN

I popped a headphone out when I heard the high-pitched squealing noise coming from the kitchen, signaling that the water in the tea kettle was hot enough to use. Feye must have heard it over his music, too, because he stood up and asked if I would help pour some tea for everyone. We made our way over just as the whistling grew louder and higher pitched.

My brother, unfortunately, got the idea to match the sound with his own whistle. He saw me watching him and waggled his eyebrows mockingly, knowing I couldn't do the same.

I almost reached out with my right hand to open

a drawer to get the tea bags, but the twinge of pain reminded me to instead use my left arm. Grabbing a few bags, I gently placed one in each cup. I guess making tea was better than talking about the missing jaguar. All we had done since our return to Daniela's was pore over camera footage to see if we could figure out who had put down the trap that had captured the now missing jaguar . . . But we had come up with nothing! I knew *mi hermano* was just as worried as I was, wondering if this poor animal was still alive.

Don't think that way, A. It has to be alive.

Rubbing my tingly arm, I looked up at my brother, who slightly frowned in my direction. I knew he was also still worried about me, but he wouldn't tell me that to my face.

Feye picked up the cups and put them on a tray, and we wandered back into the living room, where everyone had been camped out for the last few hours, watching multiple screens.

Everyone thanked us as we placed their steaming cups by them, before settling down at our own little workstation. I pressed play on the grainy black-and-white video we had been watching before. I popped my headphones back in, listening to some upbeat pop music and bopping my head along to the tune. It couldn't have been more than a few seconds after the song had finished before Leo jumped up next to me, holding up his tablet and pointing wildly at it.

"I got something!" Leo yelped, a big smile on his face.

"*¡Déjame ver!*" Mónica pleaded, jumping up next to her brother and trying to steal the screen away from her sibling with no luck. "Let me see!"

A tall figure swooped in to grab the tablet out of Leo's hands, causing him to stop jumping and pout.

"Who deployed the tall Australian on me?!" he asked, now pointing to Connor, who was grinning and passing the screen to our parents. "Not fair!"

"Leo! This is great!" my mom said, a huge smile

on her face. She passed the tablet around for us to see what one of the cameras had captured: a poor-quality photo of a dark hat.

"Does anyone recognize that hat?" Mark asked, looking around at us. We all shook our heads.

"Can I see that real quick?" I asked, wanting to take a closer look. Something seemed vaguely familiar about it and my gut was telling me to *really* look at the hat.

Mónica passed it over to me, and as soon as I saw the photo closer, I gasped.

"Feye," I breathed, not believing what I was seeing. From the quick glance I had gotten before, it had looked like a regular dark hat with some light stuff on the front. But up close, I could see a logo clearly visible. A logo that was familiar to us.

We had seen it on the clothes of the couple who had found us near the crocodile nest.

I had seen it on them again in Sri Lanka when they were trying to grab the Pondicherry shark.

And now I was seeing it here . . . were they following us?

"No way . . ." Feye whispered, and we both looked up at each other with the same question in our eyes. *What is going on?!*

"Kids, are you okay?" Alice asked, concern clouding her face.

"Yeah, Adrianna, you look really pale," Mónica agreed, her words tinged with worry.

"We . . . know who that is," Feye said, looking at our parents.

"You do?!" Dad asked, crossing the room to reach us. "Is it someone we've met here?"

I shook my head. "We actually recognize that hat from multiple places," I said. "We don't actually know the person—the people—who wear it."

And then Feye and I began to tell our parents about our experience with the poachers in Cuba, and again in Sri Lanka.

My dad frowned. "I wish you would have told us

about this before—" my dad started to say, but Mr. Savage cut him off.

"All we see is a hat here. How can we be certain it's the same people you've seen before?"

"That's true, it's a hat with a logo and we aren't seeing any faces," Mark said, mulling it over. "Anyone could have stuff with that logo on it—do we know what it stands for? Is it a brand?"

"Ask Mr. Savage," Feye said. "He has stuff with that logo on it."

We all turned to Mr. Savage. It could have just been a trick of the light, but I could have sworn he paled a bit.

He shrugged before answering, "I do. It's from a . . . fish and wildlife shop somewhere in the States."

"Well, that's kind of a dead end, then," Mark said. "A lot of other people could have bought similar stuff and be running around with this logo. The police are going to need more than this."

"But Adrianna has seen their faces twice before, not just the logo," my dad countered. "People having the same stuff from a shop is one thing, but the same face is a different thing."

Mark looked thoughtful for a second and then nodded. "True," he replied.

"No offense to the kids," Mr. Savage said. "But children's memories aren't exactly as reliable as an adult's."

I opened my mouth to make an angry retort, but Connor jumped in first.

"Well, I'm not a kid and I can verify that Feye and Adrianna encountered them in Cuba. We passed them in our boat the night that Adrianna and Feye rescued the crocodile eggs," he said. "I remember they were wearing clothes with this logo on them. Are you saying my memory isn't reliable, Rick?"

Mr. Savage turned a deep shade of crimson and let out some words I couldn't quite make out.

"I believe in my kids," Mom said. "If they said they've seen these people twice before, then that's the truth."

She turned to give us a hug. "I'm so sorry you felt

like you couldn't have come to us sooner with this information," she mumbled into our heads, planting kisses on us.

"You wouldn't have believed us without any proof," Feye said. "Which is why A was trying to get a picture of them in Sri Lanka."

"You're right, we probably wouldn't have believed you without some more information . . . but please know that we believe you now," Dad reassured us, and we wrapped him up in our family hug.

"What happened to the jaguar . . . Is that our fault?" I asked, finally voicing the growing pit of guilt that I felt in my stomach.

"No!" everyone said together.

"These people are responsible for their own actions. This is not your fault," Daniela said in a warm tone, and she gave me a small smile. Leo and Mónica were lucky to have her as their mom.

I could see Connor looking at the video. He fiddled with the tablet. "Do you see their faces in other parts of the video?"

I suddenly grew hopeful that they had stepped far enough away from the camera for us to see what they looked like. If it wasn't the poachers we'd seen before, who else would it be?

Connor replayed the video, sliding the noise volume bar over to 100 percent.

And then we heard it. It was faint, as if the microphone had been covered up or away from where their voices were, but I could hear those unmistakable accents. My body erupted into goose bumps.

"That's them!" I cried. "I would recognize their voices anywhere! That's definitely them!"

Feye nodded in agreement.

"Well, then there is the proof that it's the same people," Mónica said.

"But why are they following you guys?" Leo asked.

Nobody answered. That was the million-dollar question, huh?

"I still feel like this is my fault and I should have said something earlier!" I said, throwing my hands up in the air in frustration.

"Well, there's one way to help you not feel that way," Mom said, picking up her phone and pressing some buttons on the screen before we all heard it start to ring. "We can now tell someone what we know and do something about it."

CHAPTER SIXTEEN

The next morning, someone knocked on the door just as we were finishing breakfast. With my good arm, I opened the door to be greeted by a tall man in a polished navy uniform. The sun glinted off his golden medals. He was a Mexican police officer. Taking off his matching dark blue hat, he looked a bit surprised to see me and then looked above me, almost as if asking where my parents were.

"They're in the *sala*," I said, moving aside to give him room to enter the house and see everyone gathered in the living room. Well, almost everyone. Mr. Savage had excused himself to go into town and handle some business for the show.

"*Hola, mi nombre es Rey,*" the policeman said,

introducing himself. Judging by the purple moons under his eyes, I doubted he was getting much sleep. Being a police officer who dealt with wildlife trafficking had to be tough.

"*Gracias* for coming, Officer Rey," Daniela started, and then began introducing herself and her work. When she finished, our parents explained why we were here and told them a little bit of what Feye and I had said.

"But really, you should ask Adrianna and Feye about the poachers since they are the ones who have seen them the most," Dad said, motioning us forward with his hand.

I didn't realize how tough it would be to do the right thing, especially when it meant speaking my truth in front of so many grown-ups. For some kids, standing up for themselves was super easy . . . but to be honest, I kind of found it intimidating. But I knew how important this was, and in our household, our voices always counted, even if we didn't always agree.

This was my time to make sure my voice was heard.

As the officer turned his attention to me, I told him everything I could remember about the poachers. How Mr. Muscle Lucky Charms always wore a black hat and had suntanned skin that was covered in dark tattoos. How his partner in crime had long, light blonde hair and pale skin. Their voices, their eyes, their accents . . . everything.

Well, almost everything.

I left out the part about Mr. Savage and his possible connection to the poachers because I didn't have any proof. And while my opinion was important, I knew I had to back an accusation like that with some hard facts.

"They're dangerous and mean," Feye finished saying. "They've almost hurt my sister and they need to be stopped."

I looked up at him and gave him a smile. My protective big brother.

"Officer Rey, it is vital that we rescue this jaguar. Jaguars are trafficked for their fangs, claws, heads, and more. If this poor animal gets in the wrong hands, it's done for!" Daniela said, a little bit of panic in her voice.

I shook my head. I couldn't imagine the beautiful jaguar being treated that way.

"Unfortunately, your cat isn't the only report we've had of a jaguar landing in poachers' hands." Officer Rey sighed, running his hand through his thick black hair. "We are seeing this illegal trade throughout the continent . . . It's obviously a highly organized crime scheme."

"How bad is it?" Feye asked, curious.

"Well, we're worried that a profitable market could spring up for jaguar parts—we have already seen it happen to other animals, like the totoaba and the vaquita," the officer replied. "It can get out of hand, and that isn't good news for any wildlife."

Totoaba? Why did that name sound familiar . . . ?

I wriggled out of my dad's lap and reached for my field notebook, flipping the pages until I saw what I was looking for. Side by side, there were the

TOTOABA

- Large species of fish native to the Gulf of California in Mexico.
- It can grow up to approximately six feet in length and weigh 220 pounds.
- On the IUCN Red List of Threatened Species as "critically endangered."
- Hunted for its swim bladder (responsible for maintaining buoyancy), which is considered a delicacy in some parts of Asia.

vaquita and the totoaba. When had I written that one down?!

I looked up from my quick reading to hear Daniela say that Mexico needed urgent legislation to classify killing a jaguar as a "serious crime," and my mom agreed, saying that illegal wildlife trade officials recently echoed that same thought.

"So how do you propose we recapture the jaguar?" Dad asked.

"In the past, we've set up a trap of sorts for poachers," the officer said. "We'd start a rumor about a rare animal in a defined location, and then wait for the poachers to try and take it. But I have to warn you, this kind of thing doesn't always work. And there's no guarantee that the jaguar they've already taken is still alive."

My stomach lurched.

Officer Rey stared around at our solemn faces. "I don't have a giant staff like some wildlife enforcement agencies. Or a lot of money for surveillance equipment."

After a few beats of silence, it was Feye who excitedly let out an "Oh!" and held up his phone.

"We have people! And lots of cameras!" he exclaimed.

"What?" Mom asked, her eyebrows scrunching up in confusion.

"The hidden camera traps we use to capture jaguar movements . . . What if we use them to capture another kind of predator's movements?" Feye asked, mimicking his phone to take photos. "We can record the poachers in action!"

"That . . . isn't a bad idea," Officer Rey said. "If you're willing to use your cameras for this."

"Of course! The cameras are already set up," Daniela agreed. "We just need to set them up to send us their feed in live time instead of getting the footage at the end of the night."

"Can you do that?" Leo asked, craning his neck to look up in awe. His mom winked.

"I know a guy," she said, and then got up as

she whipped her phone out of her back pocket and started dialing a number.

"Hey, Brandon, how are you?" is all I heard before she disappeared into another room.

"But how do we get the poachers to come to a specific spot in this vast forest?" my dad asked. "We can't turn every camera on live, surely."

"We need bait!" Feye said, a smile on his face. Someone had watched too many crime shows!

"Meat isn't going to attract them," Mónica teased, sticking her tongue out.

"No, we need a jaguar," Feye replied. "It's like Officer Rey said, they need to hear about a special jaguar in a specific area."

The small chatter that was happening in the room stopped as all eyes turned to Feye. It was a good thing Daniela hadn't been here to listen to his idea!

"You want to put another jaguar in harm's way?" I asked, looking at my brother in confusion. This wasn't guaranteed to work, and we could lose this jaguar, too!

"We would be nearby and monitor the whole situation, right, Officer Rey?" Feye asked, turning to look at the police officer.

"Feye has a point," Mom said slowly.

Dad and I whipped our heads to look at her as we both said, "He *what*?!"

"Officer Rey, you can see how many willing volunteers you have here," my mom said. "Realistically, how many officers from your end would be available to help protect the jaguar?"

He shrugged. "Maybe ten, if I call in some favors. Like I said, we don't have a full-fledged division dedicated to this sort of stuff here, unfortunately. Small town, you know?"

We all nodded. We knew.

Daniela, now back from her call, happily announced she was getting fifteen cameras in the area to transmit their feed live to her computers. We would just need to go and manually reset the cameras.

Now, with Officer Rey's and Daniela's help, we

just had to decide what area of the reserve to lure the poachers to.

"If we have the area on a tight perimeter, there is no way they would be able to escape, thanks to the mountain," Officer Rey explained, pointing at the paper map we were gathered around.

Daniela *hmm*-ed for a second, mulling the countless decisions that were probably flying through her head.

Feye gave me a sly smile. Show-off. I stuck my tongue out at him and he returned the gesture before Dad told us to knock it off.

"I think it could work," Daniela said. All the adults started talking logistics as the front door swung wide open, revealing Mr. Savage looking slightly out of breath.

"Why are there police here?" he asked in between pants. "I thought you were just making a phone report?"

After he sat down with some cold water, he

listened to Feye's idea and how Officer Rey planned to execute it with our help.

"I don't like it," Mr. Savage said after everyone had stopped talking. He stood up and straightened his shirt, his mouth in a thin line of disapproval.

"Really, Rick?" Connor asked. "*You* don't like the idea of this huge undercover operation? It's TV gold!"

"This isn't going to fit in with the rest of the episode," Mr. Savage said, sputtering. "We're supposed to be capturing the majesty of nature, not showing a bunch of grainy footage of hats."

"What does that even mean?" Mark asked.

He seemed genuinely confused, but I wasn't. It was clear that Mr. Savage wanted us to leave the poachers alone. There could only be one reason that he wanted us to walk away from what could be our best episode yet. I'd had my suspicions before, but now I was certain: He was somehow involved with this poaching scheme.

"The cameras are already there, Rick, so they should be used for good," Alice replied.

"Think of the footage we could get," Dad said. "It'll make excellent TV if we capture them!"

It was like watching a tennis match between the adults, with Mr. Savage serving everyone excuses and them tossing answers right back at a pace he couldn't possibly keep up with.

He wasn't going to win. Everyone was on board except him for no reason, unless it was that he was terrified of those poachers being caught and ratting him out.

"The only hiccup is if the cameras stop transmitting. Otherwise, it's a solid plan," Daniela finally said, as if ending the argument.

I saw Mr. Savage tense up. Looking closely, I spotted the corners of his mouth slightly upturned in a smile. He must have felt me looking at him closely because his poker face slid back into place.

"Yes, Adrianna?" he asked. "Something to say?"

I felt like he was waiting for me to blurt something out about him and have my parents kick me off this mission. But I wouldn't give him that satisfaction. Instead, I plastered on my own poker face—a sweet, innocent smile.

"Not at all, Mr. Savage," I replied, looking away but still able to see his frown out of the corner of my eye.

"Then it's settled. Tomorrow, we catch ourselves some poachers," Officer Rey announced.

CHAPTER SEVENTEEN

Bright and early the next morning, we were back in the forest. If we thought it was going to be easy to find a bunch of camouflaged trail cameras, we were kidding ourselves. They were designed to blend into their surroundings, their plastic coverings painted to look like tree bark that was flaking off, and able to capture jaguars at any time of the day. And while animals can hear the sound of the cameras and see the infrared illumination . . . we humans? Not so much. Even though we had the coordinates for each camera, it was still a lot of staring at trees to figure out where they were.

"This is going to be impossible," Leo said, adjusting his arm in his sling for the fifth time since we had split up from our parents to look for the cameras. Static chatter over the walkie-talkies shared the news that our parents had already found three cameras, while the camera crew had found two. Us?

A big, fat zero.

Leo let out a grunt of frustration and then tossed the sling into his backpack, opting to just have his arm in the cast hang limply by his side.

"Nah, I'm sure we will be able to find some . . ." I said. Spring green grass covered some bumps and hollows of the area we were in, with rich brown dirt peeking beneath decaying leaves and scattered branches. The breeze trickled through the leaves, causing some to flutter down toward us.

"I think I found one!" Feye cried, followed by laughter from Mónica as she chased after him to get there first.

I couldn't stop the smile that was slowly spreading across my face. This was such a wonderful place, no wonder the jaguars loved it! Standing in one spot, I looked up at the treetops and spun in a slow circle to make sure I took in every detail, cataloguing the light and colors to be tucked away in some part of my brain. I uncapped my camera and took a few pictures of the surrounding area.

But the snapping of twigs brought me back to reality. Mr. Savage had stepped out of the trees. I watched as he unlocked a camera box and began fiddling with it. It looked different from the others, but I couldn't quite place why. My thoughts became scattered as my throat welled, remembering why we were here . . . because it *wasn't* safe for jaguars, no matter how much they loved it.

I gritted my teeth. Why was he even here? Wasn't he supposed to be with the camera crew?

"Look, A! Up there!" Leo said, running way out in front of me to point out a camouflaged camera box. With their built-in motion sensors, the camera was probably going wild and taking photos of us approaching it. So much for avoiding "false triggers."

"Go get it, Leo!" I cheered him on as he scrambled to unlock the case. He put a small device into the SD slot that would allow Daniela's friend to livestream the feed instead of just capturing still images or videos we would later have to collect. Each of us had a handful of these devices, to make sure all the traps would have one.

With a final click, the camera light turned green, showing that it was now in live mode. Perfect!

Jogging up to him, I gave him a high five on his good hand, and we went to catch up to our siblings.

I spotted my brother as he offered his hand to Mónica so she could jump over a particularly muddy puddle. Where had these manners come from?

Just ahead of them, I could barely make out a red light in between all the green surroundings. I left Leo in the dust as I sprinted ahead to change this camera by myself.

"Well, Adrianna has definitely not found one!" Feye called out with some sarcasm in his voice as I zoomed past him and Mónica.

Reaching my intended target, I tried to tug apart the box without being in the camera frame, even though I could hear a faint clicking noise every time my finger brushed near the lens. When it finally came loose with a *pop!* noise, my free hand dug into my right pocket to locate one of the small chips.

The camera was just tall enough that I would have to be on my tiptoes to properly get the job done. I carefully pinched the chip in between two fingers and struggled to insert it into the slot. After a few seconds of completely missing it, I stepped back, looked to see where it was, and then tried it again.

Got it!

"Aw, dang it, Mr. S, you're too good! This is the second one you've found!" Mónica laughed from behind me. I cringed at the sound of his name. Turning around, I saw that Mr. Savage was fiddling with another camera. The green live light or its regular red light weren't visible . . . meaning it was completely off.

Had he done that?

I had just taken a picture of this whole space, so

that meant maybe I had captured the camera before he got to it, too!

I grabbed it from my back pocket, turned it back on, and flicked to the picture gallery. After a few seconds of zooming in on every picture, I was able to spot the camera trap . . . and it had a red light on!

Meaning either it had malfunctioned right before Mr. Savage touched it . . . or he had purposely switched it off.

Looking up, I could see Mr. Savage was too engrossed in whatever he was doing to notice me snapping a picture of him. The forest had been alive with music before, so the click should have been little more than a whisper. But a twig cracked under my boot, as loud as lightning, and Mr. Savage whirled around just as I shoved the camera behind me. His eyes locked onto mine, his nostrils flared.

"What are you doing, Adrianna?" Mr. Savage asked. A quiet, curious question. He stepped toward me and I backed up a few inches.

"My parents told me to double-check all the cameras here," I said with a smile, knowing I had caught him red-handed in a potential act of sabotage. "That one seems to be off for some reason . . . maybe it's malfunctioning? I took a picture of the area so I could remember which camera it was. Maybe we can get someone over here to check them before tonight."

Mr. Savage clearly didn't believe me, but before he could say more, my parents strolled into the clearing.

I waved them over. "One of these cameras seems to be broken," I said. "We'd better give it a once-over." I gestured to the camera that Mr. Savage had just been tinkering with.

"That won't be necessary!" Mr. Savage said. "It seems just fine to me."

"Oh," I replied sweetly. "I think it's *very* necessary. We don't want to miss *anything*." I grinned as Mr. Savage stalked back through the forest in the direction of the van.

CHAPTER EIGHTEEN

As night fell, we all gathered by the cars to check in. Officer Rey and most of his team had already fanned out into the forest, surrounding the area we'd pinpointed on the map. He left a few officers back with us to help monitor the camera feeds, confident we would catch the poachers tonight. Apparently, the cops had fed out a rumor that the infamous black jaguar had been seen on these cameras the last few nights. What a great idea . . . why hadn't we thought of it?

"Are all the cameras switched to live mode?" Daniela asked, her normally soft eyes hardened with the importance of our mission. If we didn't pull this off, not only would we miss our chance to catch the poachers, but we could also lose the young jaguar we had gotten permission to borrow from the local sanctuary.

I didn't like the idea of using the jaguar as bait, but the adults had gotten together and made that decision. If you asked me, the risk was too great . . . especially with poachers who seemed to disappear better than any magician I'd ever seen.

The crew in the van nodded, except Mr. Savage, who just stared out the window. I narrowed my eyes at him. I hoped that he hadn't somehow found a way to tip off the poachers. But he must have thought that they were still coming tonight—or why would he have bothered trying to tamper with the cameras?

I had wanted to show my parents the photos I'd taken, and explain what I thought Mr. Savage had been doing. But when I flipped through the photo library, everything had come out blurry. *UGH!* But I knew what I had seen. I'd get another chance to fill my parents in about Mr. Savage, I just knew it.

"You're awfully quiet for such an exciting mission, Rick!" Connor said.

Mr. Savage shrugged. "A lot is at stake here . . ." he said.

Dad nodded. "He's right. We have to get this right or we'll lose the poachers."

I didn't think that's what Mr. Savage meant, but I didn't want to burst Dad's bubble.

"Let's go over everything again," Mom said. Daniela nodded in agreement, and both looked at the officers who were leaning on the open door of our vehicle.

"We have a few ongoing tactics," one of the officers said, holding up a finger. "The first is we've taken all of this past week's footage from the camera traps you've given us—"

"Wait, what?!" Mr. Savage interrupted. "You turned over footage without clearing it with me first?"

Everyone turned to look at him, their eyebrows raised.

Daniela looked confused. Her brow furrowed. "I didn't need to clear it with anyone. I gave them the footage from *my* camera traps."

"Well, I still would have liked a heads-up," Mr Savage huffed. "What if they bar us from using it on the show?"

"You can't just swoop in and claim all my hard work as your property, Rick," Daniela continued. "I signed up to help Julio and Evelyn capture an injured jaguar for rehabilitation, not for whatever parachute science scheme you seem to be cooking up."

Mr. Savage's face went red.

Parachute science is when someone swoops in to do science research, ignores the locals with on-ground experience, and, when the data gets published, gives little to no credit to those who do the hard work in the place day in and day out. It was kind of parasitic in a way . . . and I could see Mr. Savage not being happy about that comparison.

"As the owner of the footage, I made the call to

give it to the police," Daniela said. "I won't have a show standing in the way of catching these guys."

"Daniela is right," Dad said. "The point of this episode is to find and rescue the injured jaguar while Daniela teaches us about the work she does and the complex relationship between people and jaguars here," Dad said. "Daniela and the jaguars are the real stars here. It was the right thing to do, Rick."

For a few beats, Mr. Savage said nothing. He finally nodded and muttered a "fine" before exiting the van and walking away to lean on a tree and text furiously on his phone.

"No signal, Mr. S," Feye called out, holding up his phone with no bars. Mr. Savage let out a curse and looked at the woods to where we knew police had currently fanned out.

"Anyway . . ." the police officer said, shaking his head. "They're reviewing the footage to see if you all had previously recorded the poachers in the area. The police van over there is currently watching the live cameras to see if they come and take the bait. Some of the cameras seem to be acting up, but we have enough. If the poachers show, they won't get away."

Those must have been the ones Mr. Savage was fiddling with!

"How is the jaguar?" I asked, knowing Daniela had given the young cat some food laced with stuff to make it a little drowsy.

"Daniela and I placed her near some cameras after we saw her close her eyes. She isn't running away anytime soon! I'm sure the police are keeping an eye on her."

I wasn't going to ask any more questions . . . I just hoped the jaguar was safe.

We waited for what felt like forever. Before night fell, I had captured several photos of an incredible owl butterfly that had landed on Connor's hand. I flipped through them aimlessly on my camera,

OWL BUTTERFLY

- This large species of butterfly takes its name from its distinctive wing markings, which resemble owl eyes.
- They can grow to be anywhere from over two inches long to more than seven inches long.
- They are usually most active at dusk.
- They can be found in forested regions of Mexico, Central America, and South America.

zooming in on the distinctive wing markings that looked just like owl's eyes.

"This is really boring," Feye mumbled.

"Hush, it's always like this on *CSI* and NBC and all those other cop shows before they catch the bad guys," I said, switching off my camera and punching him lightly on the shoulder.

"Pretty sure one of those is a TV channel, not a show," Feye laughed.

I stuck my tongue out at him.

"Think we'll catch them?" I asked.

Feye shrugged. "Who knows?"

"I hope they catch all of them . . . including . . . you know," I said, motioning to Mr. Savage, who was just out of earshot.

"A, come on . . . we've talked about this," Feye sighed.

"But he's in on it, Feye, I just know it!" I said, stomping my foot on the ground in frustration.

"I know you think that, A . . . but let everything play out. We can't just accuse grown-ups like that without concrete evidence—which we don't have! That fuzzy picture of yours just shows him with the jaguar camera setup, and he could say he was turning it on," Feye explained.

I hated when he was right.

"Our parents would never forgive us if we were wrong. It could really sour the relationship with Mr. Savage and the network . . . and you don't want to lose the show, right?" Feye asked.

I sighed and shook my head.

"Then let's just see what happens," Feye said. "Justice will prevail."

"You sound like one of those superheroes you watch in the movies," I teased, giving him a half smile. He opened his mouth to respond before yelling cut him off.

A flurry of action ahead distracted Feye from whatever he had been about to say next. We ran ahead, following the shouting. It took a few minutes of dodging branches and roots before we found the commotion. Police surrounded a cluster of trees, their weapons drawn and all yelling over one another.

"Hands up!"

"We have you surrounded!"

"*¡No hay a dónde ir!* There is nowhere to go!"

All the voices clashed with one another. Our parents stood in front of us, protective hands up, but I ducked under to spot the duo in the middle of the attention. The poachers! Caught red-handed with the small jaguar in the woman's hands, ready to be placed into a crate. How would it have ever been able to breathe in there?!

Mom took a step forward to get the partially sedated young jaguar out of the commotion, but a police officer shook his head and told her to stay put.

The man snarled like a wild animal that knew it was caught and heading for a cage. "You can't do this to us!" he roared. His eyes swept through our group, landing on someone to my far left. I looked over to see Mr. Savage shrinking back and away from the group.

"How dare you!" the man said, looking down at

the woman for backup, but she just hung her head. She loosened her grasp on the cat, who had cracked its eyes open to see what the loud noises were about. With a little wriggle, the small cat jumped out of her fingers and landed onto the soft ground below. Daniela, not caring about the officer's commands, rushed to retrieve the young jaguar and expertly wrapped it up in a blanket. Four officers lunged forward, tackling the poachers to the ground and, after a tussle, handcuffing them.

The poachers sneered as they passed us, the man spitting on the ground near our feet.

"*Gracias por tu ayuda*," Officer Rey said, shaking my mom's hand. "We couldn't have done this without your help."

"We'll take it from here," another officer said, shaking my father's hand with a polite nod. Dad returned one of his own, and then he turned to lead us away from the forest and back toward our vehicles.

As we piled into the van and headed back home,

the air between our family and the crew was electric with a variety of emotions.

How would I ever be able to describe what I was feeling to Alessi back at home? I looked down at my phone, at the message I had tried to write and had instead deleted three times now. Maybe this was just something I couldn't simply say over text. The feelings were just too big!

Especially the disappointment I felt that Mr. Savage hadn't been caught, too. But I was following what Feye had suggested and biting my tongue. Justice would prevail . . . It had to.

I looked around at our parents, who chatted in hushed tones with Mark, while Alice furiously texted someone and Connor fiddled around with the music station. Mr. Savage looked straight ahead as he drove. His knuckles on the steering wheel were white and his neck was flushed bright red, a stark contrast to his usually pale skin. After we parked, he walked quickly to his room, shutting the door with a loud thud behind him.

CHAPTER NINETEEN

The next evening, we were still filled with elation.

"I can't believe we caught the bad guys!" Feye cried. "It was like something right out of TV—and we were the main characters!"

"Technically, weren't the bad guys the main characters?" Dad teased.

"Don't take this away from him, *Papá*," I laughed.

Feye stuck his tongue out at us both.

As Feye and I sat down at the kitchen counter, making silly faces at each other, Mom's cell phone started vibrating. The shrill sound of her ringtone echoed around the room. It wasn't a normal ringtone ... A few years ago Feye had changed it to him screaming, "*¡MAMÁ!* PICK UP YOUR

TELÉFONO!" and she never changed it. I'm not sure why, but it was funny that Feye's voice was so squeaky back then. Judging by the roll of his eyes, I think it slightly annoyed him.

Feye slid the phone across the counter toward her, and she quickly glanced at the number. Cradling the mobile between her ear and shoulder, she greeted the person in Spanish.

"*Sí, es ella,*" Mom said as she made her way over to the sink to wash an apple before slicing it up for Feye and me to eat. "*¿Cómo puedo ayudar?* How can I help?"

She listened to whoever was on the line while she gave the green fruit a quick rinse and patted it dry.

Suddenly, she let out a pained gasp. Her phone clattered to the ground as she stared at us in shock. From the floor, a tinny voice still talked on from her dropped phone.

"*Querida,* what's wrong?" Dad said, panic crossing his face as he rushed across the kitchen to cradle my mom. With his spare hand he picked up the phone and asked the person to explain what was going on.

He listened, and then he let out a sentence of just swear words. Dad was *mad*—in fact, I had never seen him this mad before!

After thanking the caller for their time, he hung up the mobile phone and just hugged my mom.

"Is . . . is *Tata* okay? *Abuelo*?" I asked, fearing that we were one grandparent short. That would make Mom upset, right?

"They're all fine," Dad assured me. "It's not something like that. Where is Savage?" Dad asked, looking up at Mark, Connor, and Alice, who were behind us.

"He's in his room, I think," Connor said. "Julio, what's going on?"

Dad straightened up and released Mom. "*Mi amor*, stay here."

"Julio, no! He could be dangerous!" she whispered.

Mr. Savage . . . dangerous? Had I been right?

"Stay with the kids," Dad said bitterly. "Connor, come with me," Dad commanded in a voice that I could tell unnerved Connor.

"Julio, what's going on?" he asked again, not moving.

Dad shook his head. "That was Officer Rey," he said quietly. They've been going over the camera footage. They discovered Mr. Savage. With the poachers. It looks like there was an exchange of money a few days ago."

My head swam. It was what I had suspected for so long. And now it looked like there was real proof. Guess I wasn't going to need my fuzzy photographic evidence after all!

"Are they sure?" Mark asked.

"There is no mistaking Rick," Dad said, and Mark nodded. This was true. Not many people looked like Mr. Savage here, that was for sure.

I opened my mouth to press Dad for more details, but from the corner of my eye I saw Feye shake his head. "Not now," he mouthed.

"We're taking him to the authorities." Dad once again motioned for Connor to follow him.

"They're already on their way over, Julio," my mom pleaded. "We don't know if he knows he has been caught! He might be panicking and might hurt anyone who tries to stand in his way."

"Then we stall," Mark suggested. "We stall until they get here."

"Rick!" my dad called, stepping toward the room closest to the front door, which had its door closed. *Papi* turned the knob and barged in to see Mr. Savage with a crumpled-up ball of his clothes in his hands.

On his bed lay his suitcase, cracked wide open and filled to the brim with his stuff, as if he had been packing.

"Julio! Evelyn! Guys . . . the darndest thing just happened," Mr. Savage said with a smile, dropping the clothes into his suitcase. "The network called me with a *big* emergency on another show, so I am out on the next plane back to the States to see what is going on!"

"Cut it out, Rick," Alice said, folding her arms across her chest. "We know."

"Oh, did the network call you, too?" Mr. Savage said.

"RICK! WE KNOW!" Dad yelled, not entertaining Mr. Savage for a second. I flinched.

"And what do you think you know?" Mr. Savage asked, sarcasm dripping from his lips.

But he wouldn't get an answer.

Blue and red lights danced across my vision. Then the front door flew open with such force that a few pictures fell off the wall and shattered on the ground. Officer Rey and some other police officers strode in and headed directly for Mr. Savage.

Before I could fully register what was happening, Mr. Savage was in handcuffs. Then we were watching him being driven away in the back of a police car.

CHAPTER TWENTY

Officer Rey stayed behind to take some statements from us. After he was done, he explained that Mr. Savage was technically in charge of the poachers who had been caught. He had been organizing wildlife poaching on multiple continents, using his various TV show jobs as cover.

"He is like a venomous spider in the center of a poaching web," Officer Rey explained. "That web has a thousand radiations, and he knows every quiver of each of them. And somehow he has traveled in that web completely undetected all these years . . . until now."

Officer Rey thanked us for our help and headed back to the police station.

We were left staring at one another in silence. Numbly, we all just settled into the lounge room. I'd had no idea that Mr. Savage had actually been the boss of those poachers. And that he'd been using our show—using us—as a cover to try to poach animals. I felt sick.

So many times I saw our mouths open to say something, but no words came out as we tried, and failed, to voice our thoughts.

"*Papi* . . . what's going to happen to the show?" I finally asked.

No one said anything, but Dad pulled me onto his lap and held me tightly against him as he kissed my forehead lightly. That was all the answer I would get, I realized, because no one had the slightest idea of what would happen. We would find a way through this, I knew we would. As a family, we could get through anything.

"Well, until we get word otherwise . . . we continue," Alice finally spoke up. All our heads swiveled to look at her. She, like everyone else, seemed exhausted. But fire twinkled behind her eyes, as if she was ready to take on the world.

"We continue?" asked Feye.

She nodded. "You came here to help animals— and that doesn't change regardless of whether we are filming you or not."

"Alice is right," Connor agreed. "Until we get a red light from the network, we keep going."

"They're right, Julio," my mom gently said. "The police are on the missing jaguar case—so now it's time for us to find that injured jaguar."

"How are we supposed to do that, Evelyn?" Dad said, with a little bit of a bite in his tone. He shook his head. "Sorry, I'm just . . ." He trailed off and looked out the window.

"I know, *mi vida*," my mom replied. "Well, we still have some of the camera trap footage, right?" *Mami* looked around the crew for an answer. They shrugged.

"I think they took it for evidence?" offered Mark. Everyone let out a sigh.

Suddenly, we heard the door handle jiggle, followed by someone knocking on the front door. Feeling otherwise useless, I stood up and made my way to it before Feye said, "A, wait! It could be the cops!"

"I don't care," I admitted, at the door now, which I flung open after unlocking it. It wasn't the cops . . . it was Daniela, Leo, Mónica, and Señor José. All were red in the face and breathing hard, as if they had run.

"We heard you were back. Are you okay?" Daniela asked, sounding winded. I stepped out of the way and let them through, closing the door with a satisfying click.

"Been better, *amiga*," my mom said, standing up to give Daniela a hug. Daniela gave her a big squeeze, explaining they had been at Señor José's house. She told us that, according to the police, the jaguar the poachers had stolen had been found alive and was already being looked after by local exotic-wildlife vets.

"Well, we have something that might turn your frowns upside down," Señor José said, grinning.

I threw my arms around our friends, holding them tightly.

"The rancheros and I knew you've been busy," the old man started, "and since you weren't able to look through the camera trap footage, we decided to do it for you."

All our jaws hit the floor. Was this the same Señor José we met a few days ago?!

"This old dog can learn a few tricks." He winked, earning a giggle from me. "And he hit a jackpot."

Daniela swung a backpack from her shoulders, and out came a laptop. After a few strokes of the keyboard, it sprung to life. There on the screen was a grainy still picture that Leo brought to life with the space bar. His mom put the laptop in the middle of the table where everyone could see it.

Static gave way to trees in black and white . . . I *knew* that forest view. I had put one of those cameras up myself, I was sure of it.

Thirty seconds passed before there was movement on the right side of the camera and a growing shape appeared. The first few moments were a blur of the gigantic animal with pale fur that was dotted with darker roselike patterns. The jaguar was large and muscular, with a mouth full of sharp teeth. It let out a soft purr as another jaguar came into view.

Two jaguars!

I looked at Daniela, eyes wide. She was smiling from ear to ear, nodding at us and saying, "They're new! We don't have them in the database!"

"Keep watching," Leo commanded, and my eyes went back to the two felines on the screen.

Scratch that—*three* jaguars now. While I had been staring at the scientist in awe, another small jaguar had crept up to the camera, this time sniffing it with its moist-looking nose. Long whiskers partly covered the faces of what must have been its family.

Some elated noise came out of my mouth.

"All new," Daniela said again. Our parents were shocked, but delighted.

"Oh my gosh! OH MY GOSH!" I said, pointing to the screen. "Are you guys seeing this?!"

"We have eyes, A!" Feye replied excitedly.

"Wait, there is more!" Señor José said, his smile somehow shining brighter.

"More?!" Feye and I said in unison, looking at him in disbelief.

"More," Mónica breathed, pointing to the screen.

I sank to my knees, my hands shooting up to my mouth. I couldn't believe what I was seeing. Mom gaped, a hand on her heart, while Dad's hands gripped the sides of the chair he had been sitting on.

In front of us was the injured jaguar we had been looking for, dragging its paw behind it as it limped across the screen.

CHAPTER TWENTY-ONE

Everyone was in shock. After Señor José Ramón Velásquez replayed the footage for us for what must have been the fifth time in a row, I could breathe a sigh of relief.

"So, what are we waiting for? Are you going to help it or not?" he asked, tapping his shoe on the floor. Impatient . . . to help *save* a jaguar. What a change we had seen in Señor José since we first met him!

"You heard the man!" I said, rallying the team. "Let's go look for this beautiful animal and help it."

The adults whipped out maps and GPS trackers to pinpoint exactly where the injured jaguar was, while Alice, Mark, and Connor started packing up gear. Mónica, Leo, Feye, and I got our backpacks ready with snacks, flashlights, and walkie-talkies to talk to one another in case we got separated.

In less than twenty minutes, we were all headed into the forest. Alice and Mark carried their cameras on their shoulders as we trekked.

"What are we going to do when we come across the injured jaguar?" I whispered to my parents.

Dad pointed to his backpack. "Daniela has tranquilizer dart guns so we can complete a full physical examination under general anesthetic, as well as take blood and urine samples for testing."

"What are you going to test the blood and pee for?" I asked.

"I bet they can see if it has cancer, viruses, or any bacterial infections!" Feye exclaimed.

"Exactly. This will allow us to keep a vital baseline of health information from which we can continue to monitor the jaguar against as we rehabilitate it," Daniela replied.

"Then when we release it back here after it is

healed up, others who recapture it can know more about its health," Mom added.

"Will we microchip it?" I asked. I had seen our parents pack some up when we were back home and was wondering if they had brought them along for this checkup. A microchip is about the size of a grain of rice! I had seen our parents implant them just under the skin, between the shoulder blades, in other animals they had released into the wild. Dad had told us that each chip had a unique number that, when scanned, let a person know all the details about the animal.

Dad nodded.

"That's the plan!" he whispered excitedly.

"No, the plan is to find it first," Señor José corrected jokingly. We all let out a chuckle.

A rustle of leaves from nearby cut our laughs short, all of us thinking it was the injured jaguar. Instead, the whole forest shuddered. Just the wind. I wiped my fingers over my eyes, brushing away the sleepiness and trying not to focus on the darkness. I was still not the biggest fan of the dark, and I wondered what would happen if a non-injured jaguar came across us . . .

A shudder skittered down my spine at the thought and I shoved it away, focusing on the forest around me and our task: finding that injured animal.

Moving as nimbly and quietly as we could among the trees, we came to a halt when Daniela raised her hand and took a few minutes to carefully search the brush.

Suddenly, bushes rustled ahead and my breath caught. Less than thirty paces away, a pair of golden eyes shone as Daniela swept her flashlight over the large animal that lay on the ground. The forest went silent. Dad reached for his backpack to retrieve the dart gun. It was enough noise to draw a growl from the predator, one laced with pain. As it moved to stand, twigs snapped underneath its weight. I could see its paws were bigger than my hand . . . maybe even bigger than Dad's!

Dad passed the dart gun to Daniela. She held the gun up, and with a faint *pop!* I saw a red-tailed dart fly from the gun and embed itself into the shiny fur that perfectly blended into the ground and shadows. The jaguar's eyes went wide and a roar burst from its mouth. Goose bumps erupted across my entire body. That noise was pure power. I knew that if it wanted to, the jaguar could do some serious damage to itself and to us.

After a tense few minutes, where all you could hear was the soft whirring of the cameras, the predator finally collapsed. "Kids, stay here," Mom instructed, and we nodded, not daring to follow them until we got the okay. Dad dropped the backpack next to me, and I picked it up and held it close to my chest.

As the adults inched toward the jaguar and brought it out into the open, I could see how gargantuan it really was. A marvel of muscle and brute strength. I suddenly wished I could see its incredible speed in the wild. Its legs twitched as its breathing slowed.

"A, can you bring the backpack, *por favor*?" Dad asked.

I picked up my feet, which felt like lead, and headed toward my family. I handed the backpack to my mom.

"Want to help?" she asked with a smile.

I nodded, feeling the numbness shake itself from my body and be replaced with excitement.

"Alright, then," she said. "Please write down everything we say in your notebook so we can later write it up for a full report."

I reached into my back pocket to grab my field notebook and flipped to a fresh page, recording the date, time, and GPS location my dad rattled off. Mark focused on the unconscious big cat while Alice trained her camera on me.

As Daniela opened the jaguar's eye and shone a bright light at it, she began giving me information to write down. I could see the enormity of that jaguar's eye . . . each detail was utter perfection. Mom listened to its heart closely with her stethoscope.

Nearby, I saw Señor José take the big predator in. *"Es hermoso,"* I heard him mutter, marveling. Perhaps this would further change his mind about these animals.

"Her heart and lungs sound good. Everything is fine," Mom exclaimed after a few seconds of silence. She gave me a few numbers to write down, and I hoped everyone would be able to read my handwriting later.

"He," Dad mumbled as he was examining the back paws of the jaguar, gingerly handling the injured one. It still had the tight metal loop around its ankle, having embedded itself deeply into the muscle.

"Huh?" Feye asked.

"His. It's a male," Dad said as he took pliers from beside him and tried to loosen the metal snare.

My mouth trembled. Who could be so cruel to hurt him like that? But I knew I could answer my own question—it was probably someone trying to keep their livelihood safe from a predator like this one.

The sound of metal cutting metal alerted me to the fact that Dad had been successful in his mission. As more blood spurted out, Feye quickly handed him bandages to wrap the foot up.

"Time for the microchip," Daniela said, asking Feye to grab the backpack and pull out a box with expensive technology. Feye had microchipped small rodents before, but this had to be the biggest mammal he'd ever helped. With the precision of someone who had done this hundreds of times, Daniela cut into the jaguar and plucked the microchip out of Feye's fingers before burying it into the newly open wound. From behind them, I could see Mark and Alice angling their cameras to get the best shot.

"*Mami*, can Señor José help in any way?" I asked, nodding my head toward the older man, who was lingering on the outskirts of the commotion.

She looked up and I could see her thinking for a

few seconds before she said, "If he's comfortable, he can help stitch it up, right, Daniela?" Daniela looked up and nodded, turning to the elder and asking, "How does that sound, Señor José? It's not the same as stitching up cattle like you do, but it's pretty neat."

I looked at him, allowing myself to memorize the lines of his face as it broke into a grin. From the corner on my eye, I could see that the camera focused on his face, too.

He knelt down next to Daniela, who had scooted over a little to make room for him. She had already started some of the stitches but patiently walked him through the final stitches, with Feye standing nearby with scissors to finish the job. A quick snip later and it was done.

Dad had taken the opportunity to radio Daniela's volunteers waiting by the cars, letting them know that some needed to stay with the vehicle and make room for the jaguar while others had to come with a stretcher to help retrieve the heavy animal. I knew that the size and weight of these big cats varied, but this one looked to weigh over two hundred pounds . . .

Random bursts of light cut through the darkness behind us, and the loud crunch of leaves and sticks alerted us to the incoming group before we even could make them out. I didn't recognize any of the team this time, and I wondered how many people there were in this organization.

"*Mami,* is there anything else you need me to write down?" I asked.

She shook her head. "No, honey, but we'll just have you and Feye look around to make sure we don't leave any equipment behind. We're going to focus on getting the jaguar up on the stretcher."

I nodded back at her, standing with my brother as we watched them bark orders at the volunteers in Spanglish. They all shuffled in an awkward dance as they positioned the stretcher close enough that they could easily drag the jaguar onto the cloth without hurting him.

With a "Three, two, one!" they picked him up

by his paws—except the injured one—and heaved him onto the muddied stretcher. The injured paw was already bleeding through the stark white bandages, and as soon as it hit the light-colored fabric, it started to stain it a ruby color.

Feye and I let the adults go ahead of us while we scanned the area with our flashlights for anything we might have left behind. After quickly picking up some forgotten pens and bandage packaging, we hurried after our parents.

"Feye, that paw . . ." I started, shaking my head.

"I know. It looks bad," he finished.

"Do you think we can save it?" I asked as we trudged behind our family and the cameras, leaving the forest behind.

A half smile played on his lips. "If anyone can, our amazing parents and hospital staff can." His eyes twinkled with amusement.

"Dang it, there's no signal out here." Feye sighed, and I looked over to see him holding his phone up high, toward the starry night that twinkled around us. No bars. And it was past midnight. How long had we been walking for?

"Trying to take a late-night selfie for 'the gram,' big brother?" I teased.

He stuck his tongue out at me. "For the fans, little sister." He reached over to ruffle my hair. I could feel it stick up at all sorts of angles but didn't care enough to fix it—the cameras weren't on us. Instead, I made a face at him.

"What story will you tell about this place?" I asked, motioning to the environment around us. The branches sighed as they moved in the breeze.

"That it's possible for humans and predators to coexist. That we can . . . we *must* . . . think of better ways to live with our wildlife and wild spaces because our very survival depends on it," he said solemnly. "And, you know, I think that when the public sees the other side of a notoriously dangerous animal like a jaguar, it really will make them appreciate them even more."

For as much of a pain in the butt as he was

sometimes, I couldn't help but respect him even more at that moment. There was no denying that Feye was talented—both with his science communication efforts and with his photography skills, having first picked up a camera at the age of six. Even back then, he was determined to generate a love of wild animals and push for their conservation through his photos.

"I don't have to tell you that these animals people call 'mindless killing machines' are intelligent, affectionate, even loving. It's really important to share that with people, and social media is a great tool to do that," he continued. "I want to show a 'monster' in a different light because it can go a long way to ensure their protection."

I stopped in my tracks. "I think you are doing just that, Feye." He looked back at me and nodded, taking my hand and pulling me along to keep up with the adults who were struggling with the heavy jaguar.

As we got closer to the cars, everyone began

turning off their flashlights, and darkness swallowed everything.

"How was it?" Leo asked, having stayed behind with his sister to make room for the jaguar with the rest of the volunteers.

Feye told them about how eerie the forest had been, and how it felt to be in the presence of such a powerful animal. I could feel Leo's gaze on my face, as if searching for any tinge of fear. Meanwhile, Mónica's eyes were on Feye. I had to admit, they would be a cute couple.

On the drive home, I stared out the window and couldn't help but feel sad. Would this be our last animal rescue mission with a TV crew?

Would we still be able to do this show without Mr. Savage?

Would we be able to save as many animals without the *Wild Survival!* show?

CHAPTER TWENTY-TWO

I hadn't looked to see what time it was when we had left the house to drive to the zoo that morning. All I knew was that on the trip over, the sky had gone from an inky black to a light, dusty blue thanks to the sun's glow as it rose above the hills. Nature was at its best in the early morning—some animals were asleep or just starting to wake up, while others were heading in after a long night of mischief.

Only a month had passed since our Mexican adventure, but a lot had happened in that time—both good and bad. The injured jaguar was recuperating nicely with us. That was the good. Officer Rey had kept in touch about the poaching case.

Unfortunately, that was the bad: The poachers, and Mr. Savage, had all only spent a few weeks in jail. Then they'd somehow collected the money for their large fines and been released. No one knew where they were now.

I sighed. No real justice had been done. And the fate of our show was still up in the air. There'd been no official word yet on whether we'd move forward with a replacement for Mr. Savage.

A snore cut through my thoughts and I looked over at my brother, whose mouth was wide open and emitting a grumbling, grating sound. Feye had taken to staying up late each night, meaning these early morning calls to help at the zoo were "wrecking his sleep."

The car came to a stop as Dad pulled into a parking spot. He unbuckled his seat belt and leaned over to give Mom a kiss. While I still found it kind of gross that they always kissed or held hands, I knew I was lucky to have them as my parents. I reached out my hand to shake Feye awake, only to find him already blinking and trying to rub the sleep out of his eyes.

"That definitely wasn't ten minutes. Did you speed, Dad?" he mumbled.

Dad laughed and shook his head. "*Vamos*, Feye," he said, climbing out of the car.

My brother obeyed, and we all headed inside our Sacred Sanctuary and Zoological Park.

Things had been a bit different since we had come back from Mexico. First, we had a new family member—the injured jaguar! Well, he was no longer injured after a few months with us here. And he was no longer just called "the injured jaguar," since our family had each come up with a name. We put it up to the visitors of the zoo to vote for their favorite name, and *Mami's* name won—Valerio.

"What kind of name is that?!" I had asked. I preferred my suggestion, "Spotty." Let's not even talk about Feye's suggestion: "Ultron the Death Bringer." Dad had rolled his eyes at that.

"It has a meaning, young lady," Mom had said. "It means 'strong,' 'powerful,' and 'healthy'—all things we want him to be." So, it was fitting that it won. I wonder if the public had known what his name meant, or if they just liked it better than "Ultron."

As we opened the door toward the big-cat part of the sanctuary, I paused to look around, smiling. We were home to fifteen big cats, including tigers, lions, and jaguars of all ages. Each species had their own area in the open field that stretched farther than I could see. The visitors would never see this part of our sanctuary—this was just for the cats to lounge, run, and play in. The visitors only got to see the presentation area, where we educated them on these amazing creatures.

As I made my way toward the presentation area, I nodded to Alessi, who was with one of our rehabilitators, Tyus, who waved. I jogged up to them and gave them hugs hello, asking about Valerio's progress.

"He's doing good today. He found that enrichment

ball you left him yesterday, and he's been frothing over it since," Tyus said. He pointed at Valerio, who held a bright yellow ball in his too-big-for-him paws. He sank into the ball, trying to destroy it and clearly loving every second of it. A playful roar from nearby showed that Valerio wasn't the only one having a great time with his toy—so was Rowan, our (not-so) little lion! Each of the cats had toys such as sturdy balls for chasing and swatting, truck or car tires for attacking and chewing, and logs for scratching. On Halloween we usually had pumpkins for them all to play with!

Alessi laughed at their antics, her blonde hair twinkling in the overhead lights.

"Oh, he's doing amazing! Thank you for all you've done, Tyus," I gushed, a big smile on my face. I could feel tears threatening to leak from my eyes. I knew how hard my parents worked to make Sacred Sanctuary and Zoological Park what it was—a place with a good international reputation, excellent animal welfare standards, a beautiful environment, and smiling faces everywhere.

I almost forgot I was in the big-cat part of the sanctuary for a reason—a presentation! So it was a good thing Alessi reminded me after a few hours of playing with the young cats under Tyus's supervision. "You ready for today's talk?" Alessi asked, looking over my shoulder and waving. I turned around to see our Australian sound guy come in, a shaggy little dog behind him.

"Duke!" I cried out, making the puppy perk its ears up and come rushing toward me. I knelt before the dog as he barreled into me, knocking me onto my butt. I hugged him, letting him lick my face.

"Sorry, Alessi. You know me and this cutie!" I laughed. "What did you say?"

"Oh! I asked if you're ready for today's talk," she repeated.

I nodded. Since we had come back from Mexico, Feye and I had been tapped to host an educational session about the jaguars there, using Valerio as an example of how amazing these animals were.

"Yup! As soon as Connor puts my microphone on me, I'm ready to go for the opening show."

"Well, if you stopped getting slobber all over you by my dog, you'd be ready already," the Aussie teased, coming up behind me.

"You're just taking care of him until I'm old enough for my own place and I can get him," I replied, reminding him of how I had wanted Duke for myself when I had first snuck him into our crew's boat.

I just got two pairs of rolling eyes as I took the microphone and wrapped it around my ear and tossed the attached cable behind me.

"¿Lista, mija?" Dad asked. I gave him a thumbs-up. Ready!

"Places, people," one of the volunteers called out as I stood by the gate with Feye, waiting for our cue to be called into the presentation area, packed with people in stands.

"Good morning, everyone! How are we doing today?" Feye called out, both hands in the air and waving.

"Thank you so much for waking up with us here at Sacred Sanctuary and Zoological Park!" I added, smiling at the blur of people around us. The sound was deafening—I was so excited to talk to this group about our jaguars.

"We have a heck of a show for you today," Feye said. "If you haven't been here before, you might not have met one of our beautiful jaguars, Valerio." He stretched out his hand below us, pointing to Valerio, who had now left his enrichment ball and was snoozing in a tree branch for everyone to see him.

"All our big cats here live an amazing life playing, exploring, and educating guests about the importance of their conservation," I said. "And that is why Valerio is here today—to help us teach you about them!"

"Alright, start us off, Adrianna," Feye said.

"First, did you all know that jaguars are the

largest cats in the Americas?" I asked the audience. Many shook their heads, shocked.

"Yup! As a top-level carnivore, jaguars help maintain a diversity of species in the food chain by regulating prey numbers and competing with other, smaller carnivores," Feye answered. "Here, we feed our big cats a diet of ground meat, bones, vitamins, and other yummy things that they love!" Feye motioned down for everyone to see Tyus placing delicious treats around the enclosure for Valerio to find whenever he felt like waking up from his cat nap.

"Jaguars are also important in many cultures!" I mentioned, motioning to the giant screen behind us, where photographs of jaguars in ancient drawings were displayed. "They often play really crucial roles in stories, songs, and prayers of Indigenous communities in Latin America—even today."

Feye went on about how jaguars were in danger because of habitat destruction, trophy hunting, and conflict with humans. "But there is hope—Valerio will soon join other jaguars as part of an important breeding program to ensure a future for these endangered species," Feye announced. "Not to mention their conservation has been declared a national priority in Mexico, and many people are working together to study their behavior and habitat use."

More applause. It felt good to deliver such good news. I reached out for my brother's hand and flashed him a smile. I hoped we had inspired someone to learn more about jaguars today.

AUTHOR'S NOTE

If I did not dedicate my life's work to ocean animals, I probably would have ended up studying a feline predator—like jaguars! While jaguars are not my favorite "big cat" (that title goes to snow leopards), I have always found them fascinating. Growing up in Mexico, I learned that jaguars were the divine felines of the ancient Americas, inspiring fascination, fear, and respect for centuries. In fact, the jaguar was seen as a god in Peru, Mexico, and Guatemala, and the Mayans, Incas, and Aztecs all worshipped them in some form. The relationship that Aztecs had with these carnivorous cats especially intrigued me; they associated jaguars with royalty, war, and magical powers. The highest order of Aztec warriors was known as the Jaguar Warriors or Jaguar Knights—how cool is that!

Have you ever read Indigenous mythology and folklore from Central and South America? You may have seen that the jaguar plays a variety of roles ranging from a wise and powerful leader, to a fierce warrior, to a deadly monster. But if you have ever gotten the chance to see one in real life (be it out in the wild or in a zoo), you would see this cat is no monster! Jaguars are top-level carnivores, and these big cats help keep a balance in the food chain, and a healthy environment.

But jaguars are unfortunately in trouble. Poachers kill these gorgeous creatures for their body parts, and in some parts of the world, ranchers still defend their livestock using deadly force. And unfortunately, jaguar habitats are being wiped out by humans. It breaks my heart to know that as their habitats get smaller, we will continue to see more conflicts between humans and jaguars.

There is hope, though—in you! Tell your friends and family all about how amazing and important these predators are. One way you can show them how awesome jaguars are is by giving them this book to read! And while they're reading *Chasing Jaguars*, you can also research ways you and your loved ones can support the ongoing efforts to better protect jaguars and keep them safe from the threats they face.

For some of the above civilizations, the jaguar represents the power to face one's fears . . . I really like thinking of them like that. I think about the strength of jaguars whenever I do something I'm a little scared of doing—maybe imagining you're a powerful jaguar will help you do scary stuff in your life, too!

Yours in adventure,

Melissa

JAGUARS VS. LEOPARDS

The differences between a bobcat and a lion are clear as night and day . . . but what about between a leopard and a jaguar? Not so easy to point out! The names "jaguar" and "leopard" get used interchangeably, but there are big differences between the two—for starters, these spotted felines are two different species! Here's a breakdown:

JAGUAR (*PANTHERA ONCA*)

- Listed as "Near Threatened."
- Weight: 79–348 pounds (36–158 kilograms).

- Range: Central and South America.

- Love the water.

- Jaguars use their powerful jaws to crush the skulls of their food (e.g., capybaras, peccaries, and reptiles).

- Their spots, or rosettes, have inner spots.

LEOPARD (*PANTHERA PARDUS*)

- Listed as "Vulnerable."

- Weight: 62–199 pounds (28–90 kilograms).

- Range: Africa and parts of Asia.

- Love to climb trees.

- Leopards kill their prey (e.g., impalas and springbok) with either a bite to the throat or to the back of the neck.
- Plain spots (no inner rosette spots).

Both are part of the *Panthera* genus, making them "true" big cats alongside the lion and tiger. Fun fact: These four are the only ones capable of roaring!

LEARN SPANISH WITH THE VILLALOBOS FAMILY

- Mi país = My country
- Familia = Family
- Día de los Muertos = Day of the Dead
- Mamá/Mami = Mom or Mother
- Tío = Uncle
- Titi/Tía = Aunt
- Primo/Prima = Cousin
- ¡Bienvenidos, familia Villalobos! = Welcome, Villalobos family!
- Hermosa/hermoso = Beautiful
- Los padres = The parents
- Amigo/Amiga = Friend
- ¡Déjame ver a mis hijos! = Let me see my kids!
- Ofrenda = Altar or offering
- Arroz y frijoles = Rice and beans
- Concha = Sweet bread
- Guayabas = Guavas
- Un placer = A pleasure
- Mis niños = My kids

- Hola = Hello

- Buen provecho = Enjoy your meal

- Pobrecito = Poor thing

- Café = Coffee

- Señor = Sir

- La casa = The house

- Buenos días = Good morning

- ¿Daniela, que es esto? = Daniela, what is this?

- Perdón = Sorry

- Mucho gusto = A pleasure

- Hermano = Brother

- Bueno = Good

- ¿Qué? = What?

- Problema = Problem

- Siéntense = Sit down (plural)

- ¿Están conmigo? = Are you with me?

- ¡Lo hice! = I did it!

- Gracias = Thank you

- Tata = Grandmother

- ¿Qué sucedió? = What happened?

- Ayúdame = Help me

- Mi vida = My life

- Señora = Ma'am/Miss/Mrs.

- Masa = Flour

- Mi tesoro = My treasure

- Música = Music

- Gatos = Cats

- No era nada = It was nothing

- Sí = Yes

- Pronto = Soon

- Basta = Quit it

- Mi hija = My daughter

- Mi amor = My love

- Doctora = Female doctor

- Gracias = Thank you

- ¡Déjame ver! = Let me see!

- Sala = Living room

- Mi nombre es . . . = My name is . . .

- ¡No hay a dónde ir! = There is nowhere to go!

- Gracias por tu ayuda = Thanks for your help

- Papá/Papi = Dad or Father

- Teléfono = Telephone

- Sí, es ella = Yes, this is she

- ¿Cómo puedo ayudar? = How can I help?

- Querida = Darling

- Abuelo = Grandfather

- Por favor = Please

- Vamos = Let's go

- ¿Lista, mija? = Ready, my daughter?

LET'S TALK ABOUT JAGUAR SCIENCE!

I asked my friend Virginia Tech professor Dr. Marcella J. Kelly about some of the science that goes behind studying big carnivores like jaguars.

WHY ARE CAMERA TRAPS SO IMPORTANT IN BIG-CAT RESEARCH?

Camera traps are important because they work so well on large cats, especially ones that live in forested environments. Cats readily use trails and roads for travel through forests, and it is relatively easy to use cameras on these trails/roads (although it still requires a lot of hiking). Also—many cats like jaguars have unique spot patterns on each individual; therefore we can tell the individuals apart by their unique patterns, enabling us to estimate number of cats in the area.

CAN CAMERA TRAPS REALLY GIVE A LIVE FEED?

I have not really seen this yet. But newer cameras are coming out that upload photos to cloud storage or send them to your phone so that you can look at them almost in real time, if you wanted. But these systems are not being used that much yet.

WHAT HAVE SCIENTISTS LEARNED ABOUT JAGUARS FROM CAMERA TRAPS?

We have estimated numbers of jaguars in different areas. We can determine sex ratios. We can see when they have cubs and when those cubs grow up (spots remain the same throughout life). We can determine how long they live. None of this was really possible for forest cats before camera traps.

FREQUENTLY ASKED JAGUAR QUESTIONS

WHERE DOES THE NAME "JAGUAR" COME FROM? Some believe the name comes from the Indigenous word *yaguar*, which means "he who kills with one leap." Another likely origin is the Indigenous word *yaguareté*, meaning "true, fierce beast."

WHAT DO JAGUARS EAT? Jaguars hunt both day and night and eat pretty much anything they come across. Some things they are known to eat: capybaras, deer, iguanas, caimans, tapirs, birds, fish, and monkeys! Their tongues have pointy bumps called "papillae," which scrape the meat off bones.

DO JAGUARS LIVE IN BIG GROUPS? Jaguars are loners and only spend time with one another when it is time to mate and take care of the cubs. These big cats are known to claim their territory by peeing or by marking trees with their claws. The only other time the adults interact is when they defend their territory and fight!

HOW DO JAGUARS MEASURE UP TO OTHER BIG CATS? Jaguars may be the third-biggest cat worldwide—after tigers and lions—but in the Americas, they are the largest! The size of a jaguar can vary depending on where in the Americas you find it. For example, one found in Central America may be smaller than one in South America.

WHAT DOES A JAGUAR'S ROAR SOUND LIKE? A jaguar's usual call is called a "saw" because it sounds like someone is sawing wood—but in only one direction!

WHAT THREATS DO JAGUARS FACE? Loss of habitat due to deforestation (both for logging and making space for cattle ranching) is the biggest threat these big cats are facing. It isolates their populations and makes it hard for the jaguars to find each other when it's time to mate. Deforestation has also made it harder for these predators to find food. In addition, they are very vulnerable to poaching.

WHAT IS BEING DONE TO PROTECT JAGUARS? A lot! Many scientists around the world have dedicated their lives to studying more about jaguars and better protecting them. There are also many organizations who are helping big cats, like Panthera. In the Americas, Panthera helped to create the bold Jaguar Corridor Initiative to connect jaguar populations from Mexico all the way down to Argentina. They are also part of work that helps preserve jaguar habitat and prevents poaching, all while working with communities to show how amazing these predators are through education and anti-predation ranches.

SO, WHAT IS A BLACK PANTHER—A LEOPARD OR A JAGUAR? The name "black panther" has been given to cats that have dark coloring, called melanism, so it can be either a leopard or a jaguar. Black panthers are not a separate species! Some scientists believe that

the black fur could be an evolutionary advantage, providing better camouflage when hunting in very low light. If you look closely at any black panther, you'll see the spotty pattern is still visible but hard to see because of the darker fur. Fun fact: Melanism is genetic, so one of the parents must be a black panther for the babies to have black fur, too.

WHICH WOULD WIN IN A FIGHT: A LEOPARD OR A JAGUAR?

Tough question! Both are fast runners, can climb trees, and can swim, but jaguars are heavier and stronger than leopards. Not to mention jaguars have the strongest bite of any of the big cats, making jaguars the likely winner!

TURN THE PAGE FOR A SPECIAL SNEAK PEEK OF ADRIANNA'S FIRST ADVENTURE!

I clawed at the sand, stirring up clouds of grainy dust that made it impossible to see. Desperately, I tried to see if I could grab on to a rock or something to keep from being dragged too far away.

Because it was clear now: I was being dragged by a massive American crocodile who had half my leg clamped firmly in its jaws. I took a quick glance back and tried not to cry as I realized how much trouble I was in. *Whatever you do, A, don't move that leg!* screamed my inner voice as my fingers raked through the mangroves' silty bottom.

I'd grown up surrounded by wild animals. I knew what often happened in these scenarios: A person did not survive. I had never heard of someone being bitten while scuba diving, so this was new territory for me.

Play dead, A. Don't let it think of you as food, my inner voice returned, a little quieter. If I moved too much, the predator could bite down harder, making this an extremely painful situation to be in. Or worse, it could launch into one of the infamous crocodile death rolls.

My mind went back to the one time I had seen a crocodile at the zoo do a death roll. The large male tensed up like a sprinter before a race. Then it exploded into action, using its hind legs to roll over and over again until the animal in its teeth was long dead.

If the croc holding on to me now did either of those things, I would surely lose my leg . . . or my life.

I took a deep breath and closed my eyes for a split second to think. I remembered what Dad had told Feye when his hand had gotten stuck to the crocodile tag. "Keep breathing. It's important to stay calm."

I opened my eyes again. I was a little calmer now. I stopped raking my hands through the silty soil. I remembered now that mangroves usually didn't have big rocks lying around in the sand. What I needed to do was try to call for help. The fancy scuba diving mask I was wearing had a microphone. Even though it had been acting up before and I couldn't hear anyone else . . . maybe they could still hear me. I jammed my finger on the microphone button and hoped for the best.

"Guys, the crocodile has got me! I'm being dragged!"